THE HEART
OF
NOWHERE

VK TRITSCHLER

THE HEART OF NOWHERE

ISBN: (print) 978-0-6483835-4-3

Praelectus Publishing
Port Lincoln, SA 5606
Australia

DEDICATION

This book is dedicated to all my readers and supporters who have kept me writing and remained loyal to the legend of the Nowhere Pack.

I would also like to extend my thanks to Rie, Najla, Mary, Cathy, Tegan, Kylie, Cheryl, & Maryanne for all their help to bring this book to fruitition.

.

CHAPTER ONE

Nicci raised her head up, and sniffed. There was something odd in the air that late afternoon, which was making her feel uneasy but she couldn't pinpoint what it was. A small child distracted her as it brushed past her leg, and she looked down, a smile lifting her lips.

"Watch out, buddy," she called out to the disappearing form of the laughing, blond-haired hooligan carrying a bag of sweets, who was racing past her in full flight. A flock of children of a similar age were hot on his tail, their indignation in full display and soft growls on their lips.

"Bring it back, Jack!" one of the older ones hollered. "You're supposed to be sharing!"

Nicci sighed. Sharing was a pack rule, and it was sometimes a hard one to handle, particularly for the youngest and oldest members of the group. Their natural survival instincts told them that as were-panthers, you should look out for yourself, first and foremost. It was hard for some of them to fathom the dividing of all the food in equal portions, but it was essential given their

1

remote location, and the difficulty to source new food quickly.

Nowhere was the home of a new pack, formed only months prior, in the remote outback of Australia. Once a thriving holiday resort, it had been abandoned years before, and had only been reclaimed when Nicci and Dru stumbled across it, and each other. As a former nobody, and now Alpha member, she enjoyed the quiet, open spaces of the new town, and the promises that it held for her to build a future—and enjoy, for the first time in her life, a bond with other panthers. But Dru Maxwell, an Australian car-racing icon, was hardly the kind of person she had ever expected to meet, let alone fall in love with, in a place like this.

She looked back over her shoulder; he was striking up a conversation with one of the pack over the renovation of the latest house. They had stripped the place back to the bones and were erecting some new walls and internal structures, but it looked like the job was not going to plan. At Dru's insistence, things were moving quickly, both in the rebuild and in their relationship, and it was both exhilarating and scary. His blond hair was ruffled, and his piercing blue eyes were focused on the house as the two men talked. But his frown and taut shoulders told her he was not satisfied with the conversation, and she wondered if she should ask.

"Nicci! Can you lend a hand, please?" a familiar female voice called out, and she turned to head back towards the house.

Gloria, her chosen Beta, was an older woman with a wide, warm smile and a heart that glowed on the outside. But at this very moment, she was trying to carry an extremely large pot out to the fire pit. Some things had moved faster than others, and the electrical demands of their town were still an ongoing issue for everyone, even with their shiny, new diesel generators to help power some of the buildings. So the pack had continued their tradition of having evening meals together around the fireside.

Striding forward, she grabbed a handle and together, they made their way carefully.

"I would have asked the twins to help out," sighed Gloria, her brown eyes looking a bit dark and tired. "But I haven't seen them all morning. Goodness knows what those teens get up to when they disappear into the wilderness like that."

"Did you want me to bring it up in the meeting tonight?" Nicci asked, as they hefted the solid mass onto the metal rungs for it. "Maybe we can set some limits or guidelines."

"Goodness no!" Gloria smiled at her, reaching out to pat her arm fondly. "I just wish I could have had half their freedom at the same age. I can't think of anything more exciting as a young cub than to be able to go exploring in my panther form, without worrying about the rules, or getting caught. I think it's fabulous."

She pulled a big spoon out of her back pocket and reached out to give the pot a good stir. "But...I do wish they would help out a bit more. This is a big pack to be feeding and taking care of."

Nicci nodded. "Maybe we could create a roster?"

"Maybe," Gloria gave a short laugh. "You'd need to make one for my husband, too, though!"

Nicci grinned. Most of the men and many of the women had thrown themselves into the tasks at hand. With houses to repair and build, businesses to set up and plan for, and a range of activities needed to keep everything and everyone going, there was no shortage of work. But for some of the menial tasks, the brunt of it fell on a handful of members, and Nicci chewed on her lip as she wondered if perhaps she should say something about it. She was, after all, supposed to be the pack's female Alpha.

Jasmine joined them with basket laden with flat breads. She was the soft-spoken girlfriend of Brad, who'd turned up after the pack was formed, but was a great help with the cooking. Trained as a sous-chef in a fancy restaurant, she brought with her a flair for making their food taste delicious. In fact, after her arrival and the subsequent infusion of flavours, the general mood around dinnertime had improved significantly. Even the youngsters were eating better. Brad and Jasmine had plans for her to continue with a cafe when the town was finished being formed. She gave Nicci a small smile, her dark eyes flicking over to the table.

"I hope you like the curry for lunch. I added some special spices I brought from home in there."

"Well, it looks delicious!" Gloria stepped forward and bent over to relight the soft embers underneath the pot. They tried to keep it from going completely out at all times, but it still required a bit of work. Nicci leaned in to help, passing Gloria some fresh kindling and soft dried mosses she had found down by a newly discovered swimming hole, to let the sparks catch.

As the women worked in companionable silence, stirring the

pot and preparing the breads and tables, the sounds of tools and voices surrounded them. There was the thump of hammers, the squeals of children, and the occasional engine as someone moved something somewhere. As Nicci stared down at the simmering curry, the delicious aroma wafting around her face, she heard a new sound—the soft motor of a car coming at speed from out of the township. She paused, her fingers wrapping around the wooden handle as she listened to see if the vehicle belonged to someone she recognised. But this car was moving fast, and it was loud. This was not someone from Nowhere. Raising her head, she stared in the direction of the noise, acutely aware that Gloria beside her had also frozen on the spot. A soft growl emanated from Gloria's lips and Nicci felt the hint of fur rising behind her neck. The car stopped, its sleek, dark exterior tinted so that she could barely register who its occupant was, until finally the door was flung open and a smooth, golden leg protruded forward and out.

Ashley was back.

And with a hard gulp, Nicci felt her unease settle into fear.

#

CHAPTER TWO

Dru paused from his discussion with Tom about reconstructing the walls when he heard the sound of the engine. He knew that sound, the soft rumble of a racing car that he had once personally tuned to perfection to please a woman he barely remembered anymore. He clenched his jaw, and looked across at Tom, whose gaze had fixed on the horizon. When they had formed the Nowhere Pack, he had known that one day he would have to face his past again. But the months that had followed had been strangely without the influence of his father, except through the lawyers as he fought to get control of Dru's assets, and the elongated silence that ensued had somehow let him drop his guard. With the single sound of that racing motor, he felt all that heaviness back in his chest, the suffocating weight of being the heir to his father's legacy.

Looking back to the house, he scanned for Nicci. She was staring at the car, her dark eyes rounded and focused and her body tensed. If he ran to her now, she might startle. It was better to go slowly. He started walking towards the arrival, trying to keep his long strides calm and even despite his racing heart. Ashley stepped out, her long, lean golden limbs and carefully maintained blond hair tied up carefully into a loose bun at the base of her neck. There was no denying she was a beautiful woman, but she no longer held his heart. She pulled off her sunglasses and placed them on top of her head before she moved over to him. Dru could feel the tension in the pack radiating around him, but he breathed slowly, throwing out all the signs that of normalcy that he could muster. The pack was still too newly formed for them to have created mental bonds between members, so when he reached Ashley, he spoke loudly and clearly so that everyone around could hear.

"Ashley," he greeted her. "What are you doing back?"

"Oh, Dru!" She moved quickly towards him, catching him off guard. "Thank god I made it. I wasn't sure if I would..."

She paused and stared at him for a moment before her face scrunched up and she reached forward to pull herself into his chest. What the hell was going on? She was sobbing, and the entire pack had stopped what they were doing, moving in for a better look. Everyone except Nicci, who stood, stone-faced, with her arms now crossed over her chest. Dru tried to untangle Ashley, but she just grabbed him closer.

"What's going on?" He tried again, but she gave another howl. Corey, his best friend and Beta packmate, appeared. Sweat tinged his forehead and his builder's belt jangled as he strode up to them both and extracted Ashley from a grateful Dru's arms. Dru noticed the flush on his cheeks as he looked her over.

"Corey." Ashley sighed at being extricated from Dru, and then buried herself into the new, stockier chest.

"What the hell's happened?" Corey asked, his hand going up to stroke the back of her neck softly. His eyes met Dru's and he raised an eyebrow. Dru shrugged.

Ashley slowed the sobbing and took a deep breath, stepping back. Mascara snaked down her cheeks and she looked wild, yet vulnerable. "It's your Dad, Dru. He's lost the plot! He's threatening to kill anyone who even comes here to see you, including me, but I just had to come. I didn't know what to do, or where to go. I just wanted to warn you..."

Her voice trailed off as there was audible gasp from some of the pack, and concerned looks passed among them. Everyone had known that Dru's father, the Alpha of their old pack, was a vengeful man. It was also widely acknowledged that none of them would ever be allowed to step foot in their previous territory again after they had defected to join Dru and join in his plans for Nowhere. But none of them had ever considered that they would be entirely cut off from their family and friends, back at the pack. Dru swallowed hard and looked around at the people now crowding them.

Corey had gone pale, and he gave Dru quick glance. "Nobody?"

Ashley shook her head and turned to stare at Dru, her mouth curling into a snarl. "He's put your brother Michael in as heir apparent, and arranged a marriage between him and some were-tiger from Tasmania. I mean, it's absolutely bonkers! She's not even our kind!"

Dru shook his head. "Hold on. I thought there were no more Tasmanian tigers left? Hadn't their pack all been hunted to extinction?"

"Apparently not! The guy, Gus, that your father hired for researching packs in Australia, found her while he was doing his DNA hunt, and now your father has decided that he wants to bring her into the pack, so he can reignite the old ways."

Corey rubbed a hand across his face. "Wait, what?"

"You don't mean…" Dru could feel a tremble in his body.

Ashley nodded and Dru felt instantly nauseous.

As kids, they'd been told stories about the extinction of the tigers in Tasmania. The story said that their pack were once proud and strong. But they refused to hide from humans, and instead flaunted their tiger forms whenever it suited them, thinking they were the superior species. For many thousands of years they were successful, but as weapons evolved, the humans began to hunt them in their tiger form for their pelts and fur, until there were so few of them the pack could no longer breed.

So instead of making new tigers, they captured local children, and turned them, instead. Snatched from their homes or playgrounds, they were bitten in order to become new pack members. But turning through the bite was messy and painful, and many didn't survive. Those that did often went mad in the process, and became so afraid of being near others that they could only survive by living alone and hiding in the forest and bushland. For a while it slowed the hunting, but it didn't stop humans from trying to find evidence that the tigers were still alive. So the pack were driven farther and farther from their humanity, until they eventually died out. It became a warning tale for all panthers about the importance of the pack—and the dangers of humans—a perfect horror story for scared panther cubs tucked up in bed at night.

"So he's going to make Michael marry a…beast?" Dru struggled to find the word to describe them. Ashley nodded again, tears shimmering in her eyes, a small sob catching again in her throat and her body giving a shiver.

Dru eyed her carefully. She didn't appear to be lying to them, and she seemed genuinely fearful, which was something he didn't think he had seen in Ashley since she was a young cub, having to deal with her monster of a father.

"That is bonkers." Corey let out a low whistle, rubbing his chin. "I mean, would she even be able to turn into human form?"

"Sorry to interrupt." Mark stepped forward. A tall, red-bearded man, a deep frown rippling along his brow. "But I think perhaps we need to discuss this more. There seems to be a lot of information to unpack here. Maybe we could bring the meeting forward and get everyone around the fire?"

"Good idea, Mark." Dru felt himself drawn back into the present and away from the thoughts racing in his mind. He glanced over for Nicci and noticed that she had disappeared. Scanning the surrounds, he couldn't see her, and a wave of worry pushed into his gut. "Gloria?"

Mark's wife, and the pack's Beta, stepped forward from the group. "Did you want me to find her?"

"You read my mind." He gave her a grateful smile and looked back at Ashley and Corey, who were standing close to each other, his arm around her shoulders as she stared back at Dru.

"Come on, everyone." His voice sounded grave, even to his own ears. "We have some discussing to do."

#

CHAPTER THREE

Nicci could feel burning heat in her lungs as she tried to slowly walk off the fighting twins of anger and fear that had clasped around her heart at the sight of Ashley tucked into Dru's chest. The familiarity with which she had done it was so obvious to anyone watching, and Nicci couldn't stand to be there for a second longer. Stepping away whilst the others stepped forward, she strode over to the edge of the bushland and tried to catch her breath. But her mind was racing. Why was she back? Was she trying to get closer again to Dru and reignite their relationship? What would it mean if she did get him back? Would he even care if it broke her heart? Would the pack ask her to leave? Ideas and worries bounced and collided around her brain.

Behind her, she heard snippets of the conversation but the wind blew away entire sentences. But it seemed like the whole pack had stopped working and were now hovering around Dru and his ex like a small hive. Nicci tried to count down in her head and to slow her breathing but it wasn't working. Perhaps she could go for a run? That normally helped her nerves. As she took off her shoes and socks so she could transform without damaging anything, she heard footsteps behind her. Turning swiftly on the spot, she crouched down, prepared to fight. It was an old habit, and one that she could not shake when she was edgy. Gloria stopped, raising her hands carefully and watching Nicci with a concerned expression.

"Nicci, love," she said, edging closer. "It's just me. Calm down. You're safe."

Gulping down a deep breath, she straightened. "Sorry, Glo." She felt the soft shimmer of her change sitting just under her skin. "It's a bad habit, I know."

"You're okay." Gloria gave her one of her mothering smiles, which reached across her cheeks and into the corners of her eyes. "It was a shock for all of us. Come on, now, you're needed. We have a meal to finish and a meeting to hold."

Nicci paused, feeling the rushing desire to run still trembling inside. "Maybe I should run first? Get it out of my system?"

"Oh, there's no need for that now," Glo said soothingly, reaching out to put an arm around her shoulder and lead her back to the group. "One ex-girlfriend and some bad news isn't the end of the world now, is it? After all, you're a Knute. I'm sure you can handle this."

The reminder was both comforting and confronting for Nicci. Her parentage was a new concept for her, and something she had only found out about recently. The Knutes were a well-known American pack, of which apparently she was the illegitimate heir. Having been located by her cousin Jakob, she had been trying to form a relationship of sorts with her new kin. But it was hard for her to feel engaged with them whilst they lived so far away, and despite their regular phone conversations, she still found their chats to be stilted and forced. Her father was the hardest, because he refused to use technology to talk with her, instead insisting that they converse via the mental bond shared between families, which was the tradition of the pack. Having never had to use it before, the process drained her both mentally and emotionally, especially when he demanded to know what her intentions were with Dru, when she didn't even really know herself. And she had yet to meet the mother who had abandoned her as child to the foster care system. Until recently, she had assumed she was dead, but instead, she was apparently living comfortably on the coast with a new human husband. Her mixed emotions about them made it hard for her talk to anyone about it, even Dru.

"Yes, I'll be fine," she stated, as if it were a fact, even though she wasn't entirely convinced it was. Gloria arched an eyebrow at her. "I will!"

Taking another deep breath, she prepared herself to come face to face with Ashley again. The last time the two women had met, Ashley had been completely irate about the idea of the Nowhere Pack, and yet here she was, sobbing into Dru's chest, and, Nicci could only assume, wrangling a way in to join them. She swallowed hard.

Becoming the nominated Alpha had been a surprise to Nicci. Her whole life, she had never had a pack or someone who put their faith in her, and she wore the honour with pride and a touch of reverence. Mostly, to date, it had been a title in name only, as Nicci had preferred to share the power with the entire pack rather than take control, despite her entitlement to do so. But she knew with this meeting it would be different. The pack would be looking to her for guidance, and how she handled this situation would determine if she remained pack leader or became… She couldn't even finish the thought without feeling sick.

The whole pack had congregated at the fire pit. Jasmine was sitting next to the large pot of curry, carefully stirring it while her mate Brad stood beside her, his eyes watching warily as Nicci arrived. People turned to watch her as Gloria dropped her arm from her shoulder and took a respectful step behind her. Nicci wished she hadn't when she saw that Dru had already taken the centre of the group, with Ashley at his side. She narrowed her eyes.

"Nicci." Dru welcomed her loudly in front of the pack. "Come say hi to Ashley. Do you remember her?"

His question was ridiculous, and they all knew it, so Nicci flashed him a look of confusion. His lips slid into a tight line, and she understood. This was for the pack's benefit, to show them that this meeting was going to go ahead without a fight. She gave him a curt nod and walked towards them. Like the parting of the seas, people moved out of her way until she was facing them, a few feet away. She felt Gloria's hand touch the back of her arm, and Corey stood forward between them, the bulk of him giving her comfort.

"Hey, honeybunny," he whispered, joking, giving her a playful tap on the shoulder. She couldn't bring herself to smile at him, but she caught his look. He was telling her to relax. She slowed her breathing again.

"Hello, Ashley." She reached forward and offered her hand, which was grabbed. Ashley's fingers crunched down into an oddly fitting, hard handshake.

"Nicci," she purred. "Lovely to see you again."

Dru hadn't moved, the bulk of his body still remaining between the two women, and Nicci understood his stance. Now was not the time for a scene, and she, for one, wasn't about to give anyone a show.

Turning back to the crowd, she smiled as best she could. She caught Clare's eyes, the woman's auburn hair alight in the late-afternoon sun, and gave her an extra grin. They had become friends since the formation of Nowhere, when Clare had offered her nursing services to help Jakob, and it was comforting to know that whatever happened next, she had people who would have her back.

"I'd like to welcome Ashley to our pack, and in the tradition of the old ways, we would like to offer her safe haven." Dru's words were stilted and he seemed to be forcing them through clenched teeth. "But she has come bringing news from the old pack, which I think you all need to hear. So kindly take your seats, and we can begin the meeting."

There was motion as people pulled up chairs and logs, seating themselves as comfortably as they could in their outdoor meeting space. Corey, as Dru's Beta, read aloud the previous minutes of the meeting and then turned and offered Ashley the floor. Nicci noticed there was a hunger there. He seemed to be unable to drag his gaze away from Ashley's face.

As Ashley began her tale of what James Maxwell had planned for Dru's old pack, she found herself both enthralled and horrified. She had no idea what they meant about the tiger being a beast, but she was well aware of implications of a forced marriage, having felt the pressure from her own father about her choices in a mate. And to exclude family and friends from ever meeting again? It seemed abominable.

The crowd grew restless as Ashley disseminated the tales of woe, and broke into tears several times. It would appear that Dru's father was hell-bent on controlling the fate of his pack, and there seemed little they could do about it. Nicci could feel her head beginning to throb, as more and more members turned to stare at her and Dru. They seemed to be looking for them to offer comfort or support, but she didn't know how she could.

Dru looked at Nicci, and she felt his startling blue eyes diving into her own. She would have given anything to have been able to take his hand and run off into the wilderness. Escape all of this, and just live together on the basics the world provided. But she knew better. The pack needed her, and despite her independent nature, she needed them too. He stepped forward, taking her hand and sending shivers along her arm to her spine. With a lick of his tongue across his lips, he said the words she dreaded to hear but knew needed to be said.

"Ashley, you're welcome to stay with us in Nowhere. Everyone, please welcome our newest pack member."

#

CHAPTER FOUR

He had no choice, he told himself. He was honour-bound to protect those who came to him, needing his help. It was the reason that Nowhere even existed in the first place. Dru also knew that his mother had been quiet recently. Even his brother Michael, who normally would send the occasional text message to stay in touch, had been silent. But now he understood why. They weren't allowed to anymore. His father had taken away another lifeline for him, and in doing so made another cut to his tenuous relationship with his family. Dru shook his head. There was no point in getting angry about it. He was doing exactly what his father had always wanted, just on his own terms. He was an Alpha. And wasn't this the end goal anyway? Why did that man have to poison everything and everyone around him? What bitterness had led him to be this way? He squeezed Nicci's hand, the warmth of it feeling like the only line he had left. She seemed quiet and her fingers gripped tightly to his own.

The pack were staring at him as he took a deep breath.

"And now well open the floor to discussion, and please, try and remember that we need to keep our emotions down. I don't want any claws out tonight, please, folks."

Dru was both joking and quite serious when he said it, but Corey stepped forward and took first stance.

"You heard the Alpha," he stated. "One at a time as well, please, 'cos I have to take notes and my shorthand is crap."

A single chuckle emitted from the back of the group, and Dru tried to smile as well.

Fearful members began speaking, until the questions came in thick and fast. Nicci did her best to keep the conversation focused and on point, more than once asking a member to slow down so they could be heard more clearly. Watching her hold the crowd, he felt his chest swell with pride. She influenced the pack with such grace and poise, both controlling the direction and tone of the conversation, whilst offering sincere empathy to a group of terrified supporters. She was a natural leader.

"I don't know, Tim," she offered, giving a young man a nod of understanding as he asked if he would ever get to see his parents again. "But time is a great healer of rifts. Perhaps we just need to be patient and see what happens."

The young man looked forlorn, but nodded in return.

"Nicci's right," Dru interrupted. "My father has always had a short temper, but you forget that my mother and brother are also there. I'm sure that they will be trying to guide him to be more lenient. They also have family and friends here in Nowhere, so I'm sure they are trying to find a way through this, too."

At least I hope so, he thought. There was a murmur of agreement amongst the group, and Nicci gave him a small smile. He wanted to hold her in his arms, but this wasn't the time. Later, when the moon came out and the earth grew still, he would find her and his lips would convey to her the gratefulness of his heart. Her tongue darted out across her own lips, and he felt his body ache in response.

Ashley stepped forward, addressing the crowd with a raised hand, dark smudges under her eyes but her face now calm. They fell silent to listen.

"Before you all go, I want to thank you." She turned to look directly at him, and for just a moment, he saw the girl she used to be, the one he had fallen in love with.

"You have offered me sanctuary many times over the years, Dru." She gave him a small smile. "But you didn't have to accept me into your pack today, and for that I will always be grateful." She looked back out across the crowd again. "And I know that some of you have only ever seen me as my traitorous father's daughter, after he tried to overthrow the Alpha. But I want to prove to you all that I am more than that. I hope that you will give me another chance in this new pack to be more than the sum of my family's past. I'm not here to cause you trouble."

There was a murmur in the crowd, but Corey stepped forward and placed a hand on her shoulder. "This pack is a chance for us all to start again, Ashley. And here, you are no less than any one of us. Come on, everyone, let's celebrate the arrival of our latest member and try not to worry too much about the other pack for now. Today should be a celebration of our existence."

Nicci smiled at Dru, but it seemed unnatural and sad, as if she was letting something go. And with it, she dropped his hand and turned her back, heading into the throng of people who had moved to surround her and were whispering questions in her ear. He wanted to go with her, and find out what was bothering her. Was it just the news of the pack? Or was it Ashley's arrival? She had seemed to have been coping, but had he read it wrong?

Corey's hand fell on his shoulder.

"Thank you," he said in his ear, just loud enough that Dru could hear but the crowd could not.

"It's all good," Dru replied in the same tone, his eyes unable to leave the departing form of Nicci. "We created this pack to be a safe haven for everyone. And I don't blame Ashley for anything. Things happened, and we fell out of love. It's not her fault and I always said I would protect her. That hasn't changed."

"Well, I know it must be hard for you, especially given that things with Nicci aren't solid yet. But you have changed, Dru. You seem to be coping with this news well."

"What do you mean?" Dru swivelled around, his full attention caught by those words. A blush rose in Corey's cheeks, as he stuttered slightly under Dru's hard stare.

"I just meant that you guys aren't, well, you know, officially dating or anything. I mean, the whole pack knows about you two, of course, and your declaration of love and whatever for her at the pack meeting. But," Corey paused and looked over to where Nicci was leaving the group and heading into the distance. "I'll be honest, mate. Who knows what her family have got planned for her? Has she even said she loves you?"

The words sliced through him, making him physically wince. No, she had never actually used those words. Sure, she'd let him make love to her more than once since they had met, but she always insisted that they'd shouldn't be seen together too much in front of the pack. She'd insisted they needed to wait until they'd solidified the leadership, made it clear to everyone that she wasn't just getting the role because she was his girlfriend. But was it more than that? Was she maybe just not in love with him at all? He had to find out. It felt as if his very life depended on it.

#

CHAPTER FIVE

Nicci walked back to the edge of the township, and took off her shoes. Her fingers shaking as she undid the laces, she replayed the look between Ashley and Dru over and over in her brain like a broken record. There was something there. It was tangible, and it was more than two ex-lovers would give to each other. And it was making her feel physically unwell to even think about it. Shoes off, she stepped behind a bush and removed her clothing, feeling the soft brushes against her naked skin and taking large, gulping breaths as she tried to slow down her transformation. Sometimes, when she was especially anxious, she couldn't hold it off, but in this moment, she battled with the tingling feeling shimmering under her skin. Slow down, she told herself. Breathe. Taking another lungful of air, she dropped her clothes in a pile and then allowed the sheen to take over. As her body twisted and bent, the rippling pain that roared through her felt strangely soothing. She opened her eyes again and saw the world afresh. The air was heavy with scents, from the children who had been playing nearby to the gentle aroma of eucalyptus from the surrounding trees. Lifting her head, she shook out her fur, stretched out her claws, and arched her back. Why was it that she only ever felt normal in this form? She started running towards the old swimming hole, getting into a soft, loping rhythm as she went. A couple of times, the scent of rabbit or kangaroo wafted on the breeze and caught her attention, and a one point, a lone fox rushed away, its bushy red tail bobbing as he ran. But she ignored them all and instead felt herself relaxing into the sheer pleasure of letting her human worries drop away.

As she pushed through the last piece of scrub and found herself at the edge of the waterhole, she smiled. Sometimes when she came, there were kids playing around the edges, but today she had it all to herself. The pool was made from the remnants of an old mine that had been abandoned after they had clearly struck an aquifer. Over time, nature had taken her course, and the pool had collapsed, some of the tunnels around it creating a deep, almost luxurious, freshwater swimming haven. Nicci had always loved the water and as she dove in and felt the coolness soak into her fur and cling to her whiskers, she was in bliss. Paddling across to the shallows, she let her paws settle into the soft dirt of the bottom at the far side of the pool and she lay there, closing her eyes and enjoying the serenity of the afternoon sun.

The sound of breaking branches made her ears prick up and she sat motionless in the water. Whatever it was, it was big. Bigger than another cat. She stepped forward, out of the water and onto the edge of the bank, her tail swishing and a low growl emanating in her throat. Who was it? Or rather, what, was it?

Swivelling her ears, she tried to get a clearer picture of where they were coming from. There. The right side of the lake. Whatever it was, it was coming straight towards her. She crouched low and prepared to flee, focusing her gaze on the bushes that were now moving.

When it crashed through the scrub and into the embankment, her eyes grew large and her breath caught. It was an enormous, scraggly bear—not the sort of thing that would normally reside in outback Australia. His muzzle was covered in small, rounded prickles, and branches and pieces of bush were stuck to his fur, but she recognised him immediately and felt her heart soar. Sebastian! Sebastian and Nicci had worked together at a restaurant before she'd run away. He was the closest thing she had ever had to a true friend or pack member before she came to Nowhere. As an ex-convict and outcast, they'd both been outsiders, and had formed a strange type of bond. Rushing up to him, she purred and rubbed against his matted fur, the feeling of his hard, muscular body next to hers strange and yet comforting. They had never seen each other in their full were-forms before, and he was more splendid than she had imagined. He gave a bearish grin and walked with her down to the water, where he proceeded to plop himself into the shallow end just as she had, and wash off some of the bracken attached to him. She joined him and they sat in companionable silence, the water bobbing around their fur as a kookaburra cackled in the distance.

Until she heard another sound. The soft padding of paws, moving quickly in their direction. Sebastian heard it too, his head turning and his gaze sharpening. Nicci waited, feeling strangely less worried now that Sebastian was there, until the shape emerged from the bushland. With his sleek, black fur and bright blue eyes, she knew who it was even though he was standing downwind. Dru!

She rushed out of the water to greet him, halting when she heard the growl in his throat and saw the baring of his teeth. But his eyes were not focused on her. Dru froze mid-stride. Behind her, there was a ferocious roar as Sebastian, in his full glory, rushed out of the water, stood up on his back paws, and shouted at Dru, spittle flying from his mouth. Automatically, Dru snarled back, his ears flattening, and Nicci could feel the situation slipping from her control as the two beasts prepared to fight. In desperation, she did the only thing she could think of, crouching low and letting the sheen take over and transform her back into human form. Pain radiated through her body as she changed quickly, and the bones were barely set back into place when she stood up and yelled, raising her hands.

"Stop!" The two men instantly focused on her, their mouths slackening, and their gazes returning to her face. "Just stop!"

With a grunt and a shake of his head, Sebastian turned back himself, his broad, muscular body in full naked display. "What the fuck, Nic?" he grumbled at her. "You could have got hurt! Why would you do that?"

Dru had crouched and changed himself, and now, with a deep scowl on his face, he looked across at Sebastian with what looked to Nicci like disgust. He looked like a magnificent, glorious, amazing hunk of angry lava. She sighed internally, checking out his broad shoulders, tight waist, and muscular limbs.

"Who the fuck are you, anyway? You don't get to talk to her like that!" he snapped at Sebastian before he turned his attention to Nicci, bringing her focus back to his face. "And you! A fucking bear? You're hanging out with a bear? What the hell?"

A frustrated snarl escaped her lips. "Oh shut up, both of you! God. Men! You're so childish!" She crossed her arms across her chest. She scowled at both of them.

"Dru, this is my friend Sebastian. Sebastian, this is the Nowhere Pack Alpha, Dru."

The two men eyeballed each other. Dru, his gaze still fixed on Sebastian, talked to Nicci. "What kind of friend, Nicci? I thought you didn't know any other shifters."

"I never said that." She felt a sigh escape her lips. "Remember the restaurant I worked at before I came here? Seb was the chef. We've known each other for years. He always looked out for me."

Something passed over Dru's face, and she wasn't sure if it was pain or envy.

Sebastian spoke up. "She's right. We looked out for each other. It's what friends do."

A growl ripped from Dru's throat, and Sebastian lowered his head and took a stance that Nicci knew would only lead to trouble. She needed to dissipate this machismo, and fast.

Turning, she asked, "Seb, what are you doing here? How did you find me?"

His gaze remained focused on Dru, the large tattoos on his arms bulging as he gestured with his arms. "I came to warn you."

Dru's eyes narrowed. "Warn her of what?"

Sebastian glowered at him. "Look, can we talk in private, Nicci? I don't think this guy needs know your personal business."

A sharp hiss escaped Dru's lips as his teeth elongated. "Her business is my business."

Nicci raised her hands again and let out a sigh. Turning to face Dru, she pleaded with him. "Please, can you give us a minute? I need to talk to my friend. It's important. Seb wouldn't have come here if it wasn't." She tried to lay the heavy emphasis on the words, but she saw the small flinch on his face.

"That's exactly why I should stay!" Dru argued back. "I need to know what's endangering you. I wouldn't be doing my job as Alpha if I didn't."

"And I wouldn't be much of a friend if I didn't listen to Sebastian's wishes. I promise, whatever it is, I will tell you if there's any risk to anyone in the pack."

"Yourself included?" He arched an eyebrow at her, his lips set in a thin line.

"Myself included," she agreed, giving him what she hoped looked like an encouraging smile.

"Fine. I'll see you back at the house soon." He growled, turning away from her, and morphing almost instantly back into his panther form. As the sleek fur settled, he glanced back one more time at Seb, his mouth opening into a silent hiss, before he turned and left them.

Nicci felt torn between going and soothing Dru, and getting the information from Sebastian. She'd never given Dru any reason to doubt her sincerity when it came to her responsibility as leader, but here he was, seemingly not trusting her to relay Sebastian's concerns. She frowned. Later, she would need to raise her questions with Dru, but right now, she was just pleased to have a moment to talk to an old friend.

#

CHAPTER SIX

Rage, raw and unabated, roared through his blood and pushed him to run farther and faster. When he had arrived at the pool and saw her there, casually lying in the water with the hulk of a bear resting beside her, his nerves had stood on end. It was unnatural. Shifters had a natural order of things, and that was not the way. But when it rushed out and threatened him, he knew he had to take it down. He'd never seen a were-bear in the flesh, but he would have happily ended its life right there. But Nicci stood in the way. She'd protected that beast, and put her own life in danger.

And who was this guy? How dare he come to see her! And why did she seem so close to him? Another growl escaped his lips as he burst through a trove of bracken and into an open paddock. He must have run through to edge of their boundaries.

A flock of sheep looked up, startled from their lazy afternoon snooze, and cried out in alarm, racing away from him. He swallowed down the hunting desire and shook his head. The pack could ill-afford for him to get spotted in this form by some local farmer, especially if he had a bloody carcass between his teeth. Turning around, he padded back into the bushland, his tail switching as he went. Perhaps he should go and talk to Corey. He might know what to do about the uninvited guest.

As he loped back into the township, a few heads turned when they noticed that he was in his were-form. Dru rarely transformed in public, because he preferred to keep his strength from the others, and they were already uneasy with the arrival of Ashley. In his panther form, he was more formidable than just as a human. The power of an Alpha was on full display when transformed, and it was what his father often did to create a fear in the younger cubs—something Dru had been mindful not to replicate. But when he saw that one young cub had yipped and hidden behind his mother's skirt as he padded into town and past the firepit, he felt a rush of guilt. He should get changed back as quick as he could. He'd let his anger get the better of him by coming back into town like that.

Corey and Ashley met him at the door to his partly refurbished house, matching frowns on both their faces.

"What's happened?" Corey opened the door for him then stepped aside, letting Dru push past him into the house.

Walking into his bedroom, he felt the ripping pain of his transformation before he stretched out his human limbs and yanked open his dresser for some fresh clothes.

"I don't want to fucking talk about it for a sec," Dru snarled, pulling a T-shirt over his head. "Let me get changed."

"Okay." Corey leaned lazily against the door frame, his muscles inadvertently bulging in the process. "Did you see Nicci anywhere?"

Dru's teeth ground together and he glared at Corey.

"Okay!" He held his hands up in mock submission. "I'll let you change. I'll wait in the lounge with Ashley. We need to discuss something with you anyway."

"Sure." Dru pulled on a new pair of jeans as Corey left the room. This day was turning to shit. Between Ashley turning back up and giving everyone the news about the old pack, and now having to deal with this fucking bear, the last thing he needed was to have more problems. Couldn't they just figure it out themselves? Why did he have to be involved in every single bloody thing in the world?

He slammed the drawer shut and then felt his shoulders slump. He knew why. He was the Alpha. At the end of the day, it was his job to sort out the messes. Why wasn't he better at this? Hadn't he been given training his whole life?

As he stepped into the living room, he noticed that Corey, who had been standing right beside Ashley with a goofy grin on his face, took a step back and lowered his head. The movement was barely noticeable, but he understood it was a sign of respect, and he was strangely grateful for it. As the house was not yet finished, there was only one sofa in the room. The walls were not yet finished but there was a large, open fireplace with a mantel, which Ashley was leaning against. He had to admit, that even amongst all the mess and with tear-streaked cheeks, she looked pristine.

"Dru." She smiled as he walked in. "I just want to say thank you, again, for letting me stay."

He nodded, unable to give her a smile in reply.

"Well, this place is going to be nice." She tried another tack, looking around the room. "When it's finished."

"Look, I don't mean to be rude…" Dru could feel the tension radiating off him and tried to focus on her instead of imagining what was happening back at the waterhole. "But I need to talk to Corey. Alone. If you don't mind?"

Two small red marks sprouted on her cheeks and she lowered her eyes.

"Yes, of course, my Alpha," she cooed, and he felt the stab of guilt run through him. Corey frowned.

"Sorry. Ashley. I'm just feeling a bit grumpy. Look, we don't use that alpha rubbish around here," Dru clarified. "You don't need to bow before me. Nothing's changed, Ash. I'm still just Dru."

She hesitated, her gaze returning to his and then moving across to Corey, who gave her a small nod. Her shoulders relaxed a little.

"Oh, good. I wasn't sure how it worked. So—" A tight laugh escaped her lips. "Better to be safe than sorry, right?"

He sighed. It was hard for some of the pack to adjust to the new rules. For so many years they had lived in fear of his father, and he knew that sometimes, when they looked at him, they were seeing his father's face instead. He got it. But that sort of attitude was harder, coming from her. They had known each other since they were tiny cubs, and he had never knowingly made her uneasy. Guilt rolled around inside him, gnawing at the edges again. Maybe he really wasn't Alpha material? He didn't want Ashley, or anyone in the pack, to fear him.

"I'll show you around town soon." Corey smiled at her, his casual grin replacing the frown he had given Dru. "Why don't you go down to chat to Gloria and sort out somewhere to stay. She's the knowledgeable one on what rooms and houses are still free."

"Thanks." Ashley threw him a grateful smile and reached forward to touch his arm.

Corey blushed, and for a just a fleeting second, Dru thought he saw something pass between them. No, he shook his head, he must have imagined it. Corey and Ashley had known each other for almost as long as he and Ashley had. Maybe Corey had a little crush when he was younger, but that had been a long time ago.

"I'll see you soon, Dru." Ashley looked back at him and gave him a soft smile. "And let me know if you need me for anything. Anything at all."

Her eyes flashed as she said it, and he felt his pulse quicken. She hadn't given him that look for years, but his body responded like as if it was yesterday. He could feel his ability to control himself teetering.

Both men watched her leave, and Dru waited until she was out of earshot before he turned and looked at Corey. With a taut expression, he let out a large sigh.

"All right, boss. What's actually happening here?" Corey demanded, his voice tinged with anger. "Because whatever it is, I don't know that you want to be running around acting like your dad in front of the whole pack."

The words stung, and Dru bit back a growl. "It's Ashley turning up. It's the old pack being controlled by him. It's that fucking bear..."

He spat out his words, and Corey did a double-take. "The fucking what?"

"The bear." This time, he walked over to the couch and slouched into it. "I just went to find Nicci to talk to her about Ashley and the news she'd brought, and I found her lounging around in the swimming hole with Sebastian." Even just saying his name out loud made Dru want to smash a wall.

"Who the fuck is Sebastian?" Corey asked, taking a seat next to him.

"Apparently they're friends," Dru ground out with a touch of sarcasm. The idea of Nicci having a life that he didn't know about terrified him. What other friends did she have that he didn't know? The idea of anyone else having ever touched her made his teeth elongate. "Though what kind of fucking friend turns up hundreds of miles away from anywhere to go swimming with you naked in a pool is bloody questionable."

"Wait? Naked? Hold on..." Confusion was plastered all over Corey's face. "What?"

Dru sighed. "Sebastian worked with Nicci at the restaurant. He's a were-bear and apparently turned up here to warn her about... Fuck, I don't know. Something. Or so he says. When I went to find her to talk and they were swimming together and looking a bit too bloody cosy for my liking."

"Seriously?" Corey let out a low whistle and rubbed his chin. "I've never seen a were-bear before." He paused, looking eagerly at Dru. "Is he like...massive?" He cupped towards his manhood in a gesture, leaving no illusion what he was implying. "Cos I always wondered what they'd look like in the flesh—"

Dru gave him a quick hiss. "Shut the fuck up, Corey. I don't want to discuss the size of the guy's measurements with you."

Corey leaned back. "I was just wondering."

"Well, don't," Dru snapped. There was a moment of silence as both men were lost in their respective thoughts.

"So what's Nicci going to do?" Corey asked, finally.

"About what?"

"The bear. Well, and the warning, I guess. Does she have to leave?"

Dru hadn't thought about it. Fuck. In his anger, he hadn't bothered to stay and listen in to what the warning was. He should have. And now she might be already on the run. And he was too late. Fear flooded his system and he jumped from the couch. Corey stood up and stepped back, seeing his sheen and striking his own.

"Come on. Let's go find out," Dru growled as the pain ripped through him and the transformation took over.

#

CHAPTER SEVEN

Her relief at seeing the danger of the men fighting past, Nicci now felt strangely sad that Dru hadn't been able to stay and be reasonable. She would have liked to have been able to introduce him properly to Sebastian, the only true friend she'd had for many years, without all the growling and teeth flashing. It was nice to see him again.

Sighing, she looked across at Sebastian and then felt the heat rising to her cheeks when she finally noticed they were completely alone, and completely naked.

"Oh, shit!" She tried to cover herself with her arms. "Sorry, I didn't bring my clothes in this far."

Sebastian let out a loud, low laugh, a sound she recognised she had missed. "No worries, Nic. It's not like I haven't imagined you naked before." He gave her an audacious wink and she felt herself relax a little bit. He always had loved to tease her. "Come on then, kitten. Let's get back in the water. I don't know about you, but I was quite enjoying just relaxing there."

"Me too," she admitted, following him in. Under the cool of the spring water, she felt her body relax and she looked across at Sebastian, who was casually floating, apparently not at all bothered that his naked form was on full display.

"So how did you find me? And what did you come to warn me about?"

He stopped floating and brought himself to an upright position, looking across at her with a serious expression.

"I've been working a shady bar down near the port after I got fired from the restaurant. A fucking dump, but they were prepared to hire me, no questions asked. A couple of guys turned up a few days ago. Gang members. Some of whom I recognised from my days in the joint. We got talking over their beers, and they told me that they had been hired from some posh fellow to kidnap some girl. They had been told she had stolen a rare necklace and the guy wanted it back. Well that, and to, you know, make sure she didn't do it again."

Nicci felt a shudder flood through her.

"So anyway, I started asking some questions and put two and two together, and figured out that they were talking about you." He was staring at her with a sombre expression. "You stole it, am I right?"

She swallowed hard, and gave him a tight nod. He grimaced. "Yeah, that's what I thought. When they said you'd been a waitress at the House of Crepes, I figured you had shown those fucking were-beavers what for before you ran off. Not that I blame you. But I wanted to come and warn you. They said you were staying at some town called Nowhere, and then they joked about it. But I kept the booze flowing and pressed for more info. Basically, they had been warned that you were protected by a gang, but they have no

THE HEART OF NOWHERE

fucking clue that you're a panther. So the second I finished my shift, I jumped on my bike and headed here to make sure you're okay. But when I got to the outskirts I could smell all the cats around, and I'm a big bloke, but even I couldn't take on a whole pack of cats on my own. So rather than be suicidal, I figured I'd bide my time. I camped on the outskirts, waiting for you to show up alone somewhere. Things sure have changed for you, haven't they?" He grinned down at her. "There was a time you didn't have anyone around you, now you've got them like ticks on your hide."

"Yeah, things have changed. I'm not a nobody anymore, with nothing to lose anymore. I'm the Alpha now." She grinned shyly at him.

"For real?" He let out a low chuckle. "Well, fuck me. Good for you!" He seemed genuinely pleased for her, and it made her heart feel warm inside.

"So look, I don't know that these guys will be able to get within a forty mile radius of you with your new status and stuff, but I wanted to check in and make sure you were all right. On your own, you might have a rough time fighting off a group of them, especially if they bring weapons, which they no doubt will. But I figured one bear, and one panther, had a pretty good shot of sorting out a bunch of lowlifes."

A blush tinged his cheeks as he looked at her.

"Thanks." she smiled back. "For caring enough to bother."

"Always." He grinned.

The sound of paws arriving again at speed make them stop looking at each other and turn in unison to the tree line. Again, Sebastian stepped towards the water's edge, his head dropping and his shoulders squaring. But two sleek, black faces appeared from the undergrowth this time, their muscles rippling with each step.

"Dru, Corey," Nicci called out to them, staying in the water. Sebastian looked back at her and she gave him a short nod. "They're okay," she offered, and he moved back into the water to stand closer to her side.

With a ripple and a soft groan, the two men transformed back and the four of them stared at each other.

"Hey, Nicci." Corey smiled, raising a hand into a wave. Corey's eyes grew rounded as he took in Sebastian. "Holy hell, he's massive!"

Nicci felt a chuckle in her chest. He wasn't so small himself, she mused. "Hey, Corey, this is Sebastian."

"Nice to meet you." Sebastian replied politely but didn't move from her side. Corey dipped his head a fraction. "You too, mate. I'd come shake your hand, but I hate the water."

Then Dru spoke and she felt the ripple of Sebastian's response in the water around them.

"We met before. I'm Dru. I'm Alpha around here. What are you doing in our territory? And what news have you brought my Alpha mate?"

Sebastian turned and raised an eyebrow at Nicci. "Mate, huh?"

Confusion spread through her. They weren't actually mated, or at least, she didn't think they were. They had no mental bond that tied them together, and she hadn't partaken in any ceremony. No, he must have meant mates in terms of partners, Alpha partners. "What he means is that I am..." Nicci started to fumble an explanation when Dru stepped forward.

"I asked what you're doing here!" he barked at them, his biceps bulging and his teeth sharp.

Corey placed a hand on Dru's shoulder and Nicci threw him a

grateful smile. It was hard to watch him like this. The Dru she knew was not this angry beast that stood in front of them now.

"You already know that, Dru. He came to warn me," Nicci replied, doing her best to keep her gaze on their faces, and avoid the flushed feeling of being surrounded by handsome, naked men.

"Warn you of what, exactly? What's the big secret?" Dru's body had a slight tremble to it, as if he was fighting the urge to transform with all his might. She dragged her eyes away from the taut skin across the thick muscles of his chest and abdomen.

"A gang of thugs has been hired to find her and get back the necklace that she took." Sebastian's voice was low and thick, and felt as if it was closer to her than before. "I came to warn and protect her."

"She doesn't need your protection!" Dru's eyes narrowed on Sebastian. "She's pack. We take care of our own."

"He didn't know that!" Nicci interjected, feeling anger and frustration start to unfurl in her chest. Her brain was doing backflips, trying to keep itself focused on the conversation and not on the power and sexual tension that seemed to swirl in the air around her, constricting her lungs. "He is my friend, and he found out I might be in danger so he came to help me. That's what friends do! For fuck's sake, Dru, cut it out!"

Her voice grew louder, and for a fraction of a second, Dru looked across at Nicci. His menace dropped and she saw the fear underlying it. "It's okay, Dru," she said, softening her voice, and she caught her breath back. "He came here to help."

He shuddered, and Corey stepped forward.

"How about we all come back to the pack and we can discuss this in..." he paused, searching for the words. "On more comfortable terms."

Nicci felt herself sigh in relief. Thank goodness Corey had come back with him. The sense of reason was there at last.

"I agree." She jutted her chin forward and stepped forward from the water, trying to ignore the feeling of all the men's eyes on her emerging body. At the edge, she crouched and transformed, allowing her body to sink her through the heat and pain and back into her panther form. Looking back at Seb, she nodded her head and he followed suit, although watching him turn, she wondered if his shape was even more painful than her own to change into. With the large, sodden bear staring back at her, she turned and waited for both the boys before all four of them headed back to town.

#

CHAPTER EIGHT

This time, Dru knew that the stares and gasps were not for him. As they moved slowly through Nowhere, pack appeared from every nook and cranny to try and catch a glimpse of the giant bear who was walking casually alongside them. Occasionally, they would let their true fear show, as their eyes slanted or their teeth elongated. The youngest cubs hid behind their parents' legs, but the older ones became emboldened the farther into the township they got, and soon trailed behind them as if they were escorting a captive.

Arriving at Dru's house, they were met by Gloria, her eyes like saucers as she took in the parade.

"Well, I never!" She clicked her tongue and opened up the door to let them all walk in. Sebastian struggled ever so slightly to fit, and Dru felt himself just momentarily wondering if he even wanted to let him through in the first place. Still, with them finally settled inside, they morphed back and Dru went to his room to find them all some clothes. Pulling open his wardrobe, he grabbed the largest dressing gown he owned, and hoped it would fit. God knew he had seen enough of that man's body to last a lifetime.

In the other room, he could hear them starting to talk. They had introduced Gloria and she seemed to be enamoured of Sebastian already, having commented multiple times, he noted, on his size. Damn bear. He pulled on the shirt and pants he had discarded when they had left, and grabbed Corey's things off the floor. For Nicci, he grabbed a large shirt of his, which he hoped would cover her like a dress. If he could have, he would have brought out a nun's habit, just to make a point.

Back in the lounge, the room seemed tiny in contrast to the size of the men filling it. So he passed the clothes across and offered his room for Nicci to change. As she took the shirt from him, their fingers touched, and an electric tingle shot up his arm and caught in his chest. Her body was amazing. Small, yet perfectly formed, she reminded him of a elven statue. And as she squeezed past him to the room, he felt her body respond to his nearness and caught her scent, his lungs involuntarily drinking it in like desert rain.

With her gone, he noticed that even his largest dressing gown looked like doll's clothing on Sebastian, and it made him glower. Still, at least he didn't have to see all of him anymore.

"Hey, Gloria?" He interrupted her conversation with Sebastian about the tattoos that spread over his arms. "Would you mind going to get us something to drink? Beers, perhaps?"

Both men nodded, and Gloria, her cheeks rosy red, was quick to reply. "Of course! And I'll go get Mark. I'm sure he'd love to meet—"

Dru cut her off. "Sure, but maybe when we get outside?" He wasn't entirely certain another panther could even fit into the room with them.

"Oh yes, silly me. I'll be right back, Sebastian." Gloria blushed, and Dru felt himself groan inwardly.

What kind of guy was this, making even the grown women of the group simper like cubs?

He turned to see Corey scowling at him. "You don't need to speak to her like that, mate." He arched an eyebrow. "She's not the help."

Dru knew what he meant, and his carelessness made him tense up. "Sorry."

Sebastian was staring past them to the door, as the smell of Nicci wafted in. God, she smelled good. Turning, he realised his next mistake.

The shirt was extremely large, and did fit her like a dress. A sexy, blue-washed, just-rolled-out-of-bed-after-having-hot-sex kind of dress. He felt his body flame, and he swallowed hard. Fuck. She ran her fingers through her hair, and he imagined his fingertips following their trail. He found it hard to breathe.

"Hey, kitten," the bear said behind him in a low voice, and all that sexual tension turned into instant anger.

"What did you call her?" he snarled, turning around.

Corey stepped forward and put a hand on Dru's chest. "Dude! Calm the fuck down!"

He could feel the tension in his shoulders and he tried to shake it off. Having them all crammed into the room together wasn't helping. In a minute, he was either going to end up fucking or fighting his way out.

"You're right. Let's go outside," he said, focusing his eyes back on Corey, who was giving him a serious frown. "And grab a beer."

He let Nicci lead the way, his gaze automatically drawn to her lean legs poking out the bottom of the shirt. He had to shake his head to stop his mental images of slipping it upward.

Outside, the whole town had gathered around his doorstep. Gloria stepped forward and handed out the beers, but Dru caught the flush to her cheeks when Sebastian thanked her. So, apparently did Mark, her husband, who gave a small frown, but thrust his hand forward to welcome him anyway. They were both big men, but next to Sebastian even Mark looked smaller and leaner.

Ashley stepped forward almost immediately to introduce herself. She had gotten changed and put on new makeup since they had seen each other last, and her porcelain veneer was back. Sebastian smiled at her and shook her hand warmly, and he caught the pleased expression in her eye. Nicci stepped forward to address the crowd, and everyone hushed.

"Hi, everyone. As you have all noticed, my friend has dropped in to say hello. Sebastian and I have known each other for..." She paused and looked back at him and he gave her a grin, which made Dru clench his teeth together. "I dunno. Ages. A few years, at least."

There was a twittering amongst the women, and Dru swallowed hard again.

"And yes, he is a were-bear, as you will have noticed."

The younger and braver ones stepped forward to get a bit closer to him, as if they were challenging each other. "But he's completely harmless, so please don't be afraid."

Dru felt the hairs on his arms raise. Harmless? He fucking doubted that. But he'd be able to test out how harmless this guy was if he ever tried anything with Nicci.

Nicci glanced back at him and gave a sharp scowl, so he frowned at her.

"Hi, everyone." Sebastian spoke to the hushed crowd. He seemed uncomfortable in the spotlight, his eyes darting around them all before finally settling back on Nicci and relaxing again. Dru could feel his frown deepen.

"All right, everyone," Dru barked, his voice tight. "Enough of the meet-and-greet. Sebastian." He gave him a tight nod. "Welcome to Nowhere. We hope that you will feel welcome amongst our kin." Formalities over, he thought to himself, feeling pleased that he had managed to remember his duty as leader, despite his inner cat growling its displeasure at Sebastian's presence. He swallowed hard. Now came the difficult bit. "Unfortunately, today is not a great news day."

There were more mutterings and the pack's faces grew wary.

"On top of Ashley's news about our old pack, Sebastian has come here to inform us that Nicci is now in danger."

The crowd grew restless, so Dru raised his hand. "Quieten down, everyone."

He waited a moment. "Apparently there are some thugs who think they are going to come here and," he paused, as his teeth sharpened involuntarily, "take back the necklace that Nicci stole. Now most of you, except perhaps the newest members, will remember what she told us about the circumstances around it at that very first meeting. We have never condoned her actions, but we all agreed to support her then, and we continue to do so now. She is a good person who made a bad decision. She is also now our Alpha."

There was nodding of heads, and murmurings as some of the others explained to the newer ones. "And we know something they do not. The men coming are all human, and don't appear to know we are shifters." Another round of whispers. "But they are still dangerous men. So we need to protect her, and protect our pack. Are you all prepared to do that?"

"Of course!" A young member stood forward, his eyes flashing. "We are pack. We are family!"

"Exactly." Dru could feel the energy rising in the group, and his heart soared. He turned to look across at Sebastian, the first time he was able to smile at the man since he had arrived. They didn't need him here; they were strong enough together. She was safe. So he could just leave, and they would all be fine. He could feel a triumphant grin on his lips.

"We are pack," he continued. "And we can take care of our own—"

"Then I'm staying here," Sebastian interrupted, the low rumble of his voice rolling around the group. "Because she's my pack."

And with that, Dru felt his world fall apart.

#

CHAPTER NINE

Nicci stared at Sebastian. She hadn't seen him since the restaurant, and whilst they had always been close at work and she considered him a good friend, they hadn't really ever had anything to do with each other outside of those four walls. To hear him standing there, in front of whole pack of panthers, and declare that she was pack to him, was startling, to say the least.

He looked down at her and she tried to read from his eyes what he'd meant by that. But more so, she was drawn to Dru, whose face looked like it was about to explode. He was pale, his teeth were showing, his eyes had begun to slant as if stuck mid-transformation, and his nails were twisting into claws. But somehow he wasn't changing, as if his body was fighting with itself. Sebastian, on the other hand, was standing tall and proud, his chest out and his head slightly lowered, as if he'd accepted some kind of challenge that Nicci didn't understand.

Corey intervened, rapidly getting in between the two men.

"I don't see why we can't make some arrangement." He spoke calmly and slowly, allowing time for Dru to focus back on his face before he continued.

Ashley stepped forward, placing herself next to Corey. "Dru, Corey's right. After all, he is Nicci's friend and he's come all this way to protect her and warn her. If he's her pack," she elongated the word as a hint of a smile tainted her lips, "then who are we to stop them being together? The Nowhere Pack rules state that the Alphas don't need to be a mated pair. And you haven't mated with Nicci, either, so you have no formal ties with her. She's done nothing wrong."

Nicci felt like she should be grateful that Ashley intervened, but there was something in those words, a sick twisting of the meaning that oozed from them, and made her anger flare. Sure, she and Dru were not mated, but that didn't mean she didn't feel connected to him. It was just...complicated.

"It's not like that," she tried to interject, her frustration growing. Dru snarled softly and made everyone jump back. Nicci felt the hairs on her arms rise and her skin tingle. It was almost as if she could feel his anger feed into and off her own, an entwining of their combined distress, and Dru seemed to be losing his control of it.

"Damn right, it's not like that." He stabbed a finger in Sebastian's direction. His hand was shaky and his voice started to get louder as he spoke. "You are a bear. You are not pack. You're not even fucking one of us! You're nothing better than an overgrown fucking dog! You don't touch her, you don't stay here, and you sure as fuck don't get to be pack!"

His voice was violent and shaking, but Sebastian stood his ground, folding his massive arms across his chest. Nicci knew that Dru was teetering on an edge of something that terrified her.

"Dru, darling." Ashley stepped forward to reach out to him, but his hand lashed out that exact moment towards Sebastian and caught her, knocking her flat to the ground and causing her to yell out in pain. Within seconds, Corey's stepped forward, his normal, casual posture gone and pure menace and ferocity spitting from his eyes as Gloria helped Ashley back to her feet.

"How fucking dare you!" he hissed at Dru, shoving him hard in the shoulder. "Don't you dare lay a finger on a woman!"

Dru shook his head for a moment, the shock of hurting Ashley making him pause and his humanity forcing itself back. "I-I didn't mean to..." he stuttered.

"Didn't you? Because it looked like you did, Dru. What the actual fuck is wrong with you? One bear turns up in town and you lose your fucking mind?"

Corey, normally so calm and kind, looked angry. Very angry. His lips were twisted and his body, like Dru's before, was morphing. The two men eyeballed each other, Dru's face wary, and Corey's filled with rage.

"I'm sorry, mate," Dru replied as the crowd moved back, and Sebastian pulled Nicci protectively behind him, using his body to block the path of the two men, who almost appeared to be circling each other.

"Sorry?" Corey spat out. "You're sorry? Fuck you, Dru. I have spent my whole life looking out for you. Playing second fiddle to you and your fucking temper and mood swings. But enough is enough. I watched your father hit my mother multiple times as a kid, sometimes for no reason at all from what I could see, and I sure as fuck am not going to watch you do the same to Ashley. I'm not a cub anymore, Dru. I used to admire your passionate nature. It seemed to me like you could use to it do anything, if you willed it enough. But what are you doing with it, Dru? You're telling other weres who can and can't be part of your pack. Who can and can't be with your women. Except they're not yours, are they? You told everyone this pack would be a democracy but you're behaving like a dictator. This isn't your father's pack, Dru, but you sure as heck are acting just like him! Guess the apple didn't fall far from the tree after all!"

There was a cry from Dru's lips, and Nicci wasn't sure if it was pain or anger. She tried to move forward, but Sebastian's arm was blocking her path and it was as solid as steel.

Unable to control it any longer, the two men morphed, growling, their clothes ripping and tearing in the process. Parents, afraid for their offspring, bundled them up instantly and backed away, leaving the shell group of pack surrounding the circling panthers with fear fresh on their faces. Moving backwards, they gave room as the two men launched at each other.

There was a sickening thud as their bodies collided, and their teeth and claws found flesh. Nicci couldn't drag her eyes away as the scream she wanted to let out was caught in her throat. They were going to kill each other! Sebastian pulled her into his chest, sensing her distress, and held her tight, his vice grip not letting her move.

"Let me go," she begged. "I have to stop them."

"You can't," he replied, his eyes focused on the fight, his whole body stiff and still. "It sounds like this has been a long time coming. They need to sort this out, or die trying."

Corey, the more solid of the two, launched a shoulder into Dru, knocking him sideways before he landed and sank his teeth into Dru's shoulder. Growling loudly, Dru shook him off, swiping out a claw and leaving a large, bloody gash across the side of Corey's face. They drew apart, sizing each other up again before springing into another attack. Again there was a crash of bones and teeth, the sharp, shrill yell of one of them and the crunch of something snapping. Corey whined for a moment, lifting an injured paw before limping into another crouch. With arched necks and swishing tails they circled each other, mouths opened wide and razor-sharp teeth on full display. Dru thrust forward a paw, catching the side of Corey's mouth. In response, Corey dropped down, rolling onto his back, and trying to grab him by the throat. But Dru was too quick, slipping past his teeth before drawing a bloody gash along his stomach. Flinching, Corey moved away, his head dropping, the pain obviously overwhelming him before finally he lay down, his head dropping to the ground.

Dru morphed, his body shaking and covered in deep wounds. Blood seeped from him and oozed down towards the ground. His bright blue eyes, still in their cat slant, stared across at Nicci, who was shielded in Sebastian's tight grip before a pained howl escaped his lips. Turning, he ran out to the wilderness, his body shifting to panther as he went.

Nicci stared as his tail flickered and then disappeared in the trees, her whole being yearning to follow him but physically unable to.

"Let him go." Sebastian's words rumbled in his chest behind her. "He's not fatally injured. Trust me."

Nicci didn't want to know how he knew that, nor did she doubt it to be true, but the pain of knowing he was suffering was almost more than she could bear.

The crowd now rushed forward to the prone figure of Corey,

naked, and lying in a pool of his own blood. A large scratch lined his face, but he was doubled over in pain and holding his stomach, which appeared to be seriously damaged. Ashley ran to him, her hands soothing his brow as he looked up at her face, fear showing for the first time.

"What have you done?" she whispered to him. "Were you trying to get yourself killed?"

"He...hit...you," Corey managed to get out in between the groans. "Fuck him."

As she had with Nicci's cousin Jakob, when he had been injured by Corey, the resident nurse Clare stepped in and dropped to her knees, assessing the damage.

"This is bad," she muttered to the group. "He needs more help than I can provide. We need to get him to the Maxwell's doctor. Fast."

Nicci felt sick. "How are we going to do that?" she called out, finally getting released from Sebastian's grip and stepping forward. "Ashley said they will kill anyone who returns to the old pack."

"I'll take him." Ashley looked up, her face ashen and the flush of a red mark sprouting across the side of her face as she jutted her chin forward. "I will take the risk. This is my fault, anyway."

"Phone Roo. He'll come." Corey's voice was barely audible. "You stay here, Ash. It's safer."

"Like hell I will." She stood up, her golden hair shimmering as she barked at the crowd. In that exact moment, she looked more like an Alpha than Nicci had ever felt like one, and she could feel the stab of envy rise.

"Someone get Roo on the phone and tell him we need him here immediately. You—" Ashley stabbed a finger at Clare. "Keep him alive until the plane arrives. You lot, get her bandages and whatever else she needs to do that. I'm going to phone ahead to try and smooth things out. And for fuck's sake." She glared at Nicci. "Get rid of that fucking bear."

CHAPTER TEN

He wasn't sure if it was the pain in his body or the pain in his heart that hurt more. Blood seemed to be dripping from everything, and he could taste the sharp, metallic tang of it in his mouth. Images flashed before him, of Corey's body lying on the ground in a pool of blood. His best mate. How could he have done that to him? What kind of monster was he?

He didn't even know where he was anymore. He had been walking through the scrublands for hours. Exhausted and starving, he found himself in a paddock. With the sheep terrified and huddled in the far corner, he managed to lie down on the straw that had been laid out for them to feed on as he felt the last of his energy disappear. Closing his eyes, all he could see was Nicci, wrapped carefully in the arms of giant bear. And groaning, he let the darkness take over.

He awoke to the sound of tyres nearby. Two heavy boots hit the ground and he could hear someone talking.

"Bloody hell! You all right, mate?"

It was not someone he recognised. He tried to open his eyes, but found they were uncooperative. So instead, he tried to move, a loud groan emitting from his throat as the pain grabbed him and drove him back into the darkness. The next time he awoke, he was surrounded by loud noises. People and machines bleeping and muttering. The sharp sting of something being stabbed into his arm and the warm rush of its contents being released into his veins. A floating sensation hit him, and he relaxed back into slumber.

Finally, he awoke to the tang of disinfectant heavy in the air. His body felt stiff and sore but he could finally open his eyes.

"Mum," he muttered, looking to the dishevelled state of his normally immaculate mother sitting in the chair beside his bed. Her blond hair had escaped its ties and was hanging either side of her face, and large, dark circles lay under her eyes. Looking around, he realised he was in a hospital room, with its stark white walls and medical machinery. She sat forward, reaching out to grab his hand carefully in her own.

"Dru," she whispered, her voice cracking. "Thank god you're alive."

"Where am I?" He tried to sit up, but the pain pushed him gently back into the bed.

"You're at St Catherine's. Your father had you brought here after we got called by the Royal Flying Doctors to say you had been found seriously injured in a paddock in Queensland. They didn't know what to do with you. They thought someone must have abducted you and taken you there."

Hazy memories came back to him of… "Corey," he groaned, trying once again to rise up.

His mother's hand came down on his shoulder. "Hush now," she said soothingly. "We have him too. He's going to be fine. It's you we were all worried about. You gave us quite the scare."

"Nowhere," he tried to tell her, but she hushed him again.

"I'll let your father know you are awake. He'll want to talk to you about that," she replied, getting up from the chair and heading out of the room.

About what? What had happened at Nowhere? Were they all right? Was Corey alive, or had he killed him? Fear radiated from his chest as he fought to sit upright.

His father strode into the room and towered above him by the bed. There was a deep scowl on his face as he looked down at Dru.

"You're awake then. Good." He paused and Dru seized the moment.

"N-Nowhere," he stammered. "Are they okay?"

"Fine," his father spat back. "Which is more than they will be shortly, those fucking traitors. But I will deal with them. My men are already preparing the raid."

His fear uncurled again, twisted and turning. "What are you going to do to them?"

"Only what they deserve. Although the bear does bring about a new challenge. Still, he seems to be packless, so I doubt he will bring any repercussions. It's better to eradicate him, just in case. That girl of yours though—Nicci, is it?" Dru's blood froze in his veins as her name was uttered. "Bloody good breeding stock, that. I'll keep her alive. In fact, I might even have a crack at her myself, if you're not up to it. The cubs would be the important bit. Got to get those bloody Knutes in line, but they will kneel to her offspring, no doubt. Might be quite nice to manage the only international pack."

Anger, despair, and nausea clung to him. What kind of person planned these things? How could he have so easily let his father into the knowledge of Nicci's heritage? He needed to get out of there, and warn her. Warn them all.

"And if you're thinking you can get out here and help them, you're fucking delusional." His father glared down at him. "I've had enough of your bullshit to last a lifetime. I've got guards watching your every step, and if you try anything I will personally wipe the bloody floor with you. Son or not, you'll not disobey my orders, and my orders are to not leave this room."

Dru growled, deep and low in his chest.

"Good boy. You hold on to that anger. You're going to need it, as my heir, to keep this lot in check. But if you dare to challenge me ever again, I will break you like a fucking twig."

With the final words spat out, he turned and left the room, Dru unable to follow. Sitting up as best he could, Dru lifted the sheets and examined himself. There were several wounds, all carefully stitched and sutured, and lines into both his arms. With a wince, he pulled the needles from his flesh and tried to turn around to let his feet drop in the bed, but the room spun and he saw stars in front of his eyes. His mother returned just in time, and rushed to his bedside.

"Don't you do anything silly," she muttered, pushing his feet back under the covers. "You know how your father is, and you'll only make things worse."

Dru dug deep into his pain and breathed through it. "Worse than a massacre, Mum? Worse than the bodies of cubs piled into a mass grave of your former friends?"

She went pale, her lips drawing into a tight line.

"Well, they did disobey him, sweetheart." She lifted her gaze to meet his, and he could see the fear that radiated from behind her eyes. She had given up the pretence of being the dutiful wife, and was just as scared as the next pack member. "You know how he is."

Oh, he knew all right. He knew a monster when he saw one. "Mum, you have to help me escape here."

She shook her head, her whole body following suit. Leaning in, she whispered to him, "He'd kill us both son. It can't be done."

"You have to, Mum," he told her, his eyes pleading. "Because if he destroys Nowhere, I'm dead anyway." He could feel his heart reaching out for them. All of them. This pack had given him a lifeline and he clung to the tendrils of it like a drowning man would cling to a buoy. He had been told his whole life that he was destined to be an Alpha, but it was only now that he understood what that truly meant. And he would gladly forfeit his life for theirs. But he would have to hurry. Time was running out, and they had no idea what was coming.

#

CHAPTER ELEVEN

After the plane had taken off, carrying Corey and Ashley back to the old pack, Nicci felt the weight of the eyes that fell on her. Once she turned, they would all expect her to explain what would happen next, and she could feel the tightness in her chest at their expectation of her leadership. Nobody knew where Dru was; he had disappeared, and despite attempts by a couple of the younger members to follow his trail, it had gone cold. Shivering, she wrapped her hands around her shoulders.

"All right, everyone," she muttered. "I think we've all had enough drama for one day. I think we should eat and rest up for the night. I don't know what tomorrow will bring, but for those of you with children, I will not judge you if you choose to leave. I can only imagine how dangerous a pack fight can be, particularly for the cubs. And having been a cub left unprotected herself for many years, I would not wish that fear on any child."

A couple of the parents gave her a grateful smile. They wouldn't have left without an Alpha's approval, even if this pack wasn't like their old one, where the approval was essential.

"I'll stay." Sebastian gave her a nod. "You'll need all the help you can get, and I'm good in a fight."

She didn't doubt that for a second. Other men stepped forward, also offering their support, and among them, they arranged to do shifts throughout the night to keep an eye out for intruders. It was hard to tell what was coming, but everyone knew it wasn't going to be good.

The group meal that evening was a sombre event. Ashley had messaged to say they had safely made it to a hospital and Corey was going to be all right, which was the only good piece of news they had heard. Nobody had any idea where Dru was, and as the evening enveloped the sky, Nicci could feel her fear for him clawing inside her.

Sebastian had been a great help. He and Jasmine had made light work of the dinner, despite the lack of a proper kitchen to cook from, and in return, some of the boys went and picked up his bike and gear from the edge of town and delivered it to Nicci's. She had set him up with a stretcher in a spare room. She just hoped it held the weight of him through the night. It felt safer knowing he would be in the next room if anything happened, even though she trusted her remaining pack.

As a plate of food was thrust into her hands, she was drawn away from staring mindlessly at the crackling fire.

"Thanks, Gloria," she said softly as the older women took a seat next to her. It seemed like there were fresh worry lines around the corners of her mouth.

"No worries, love," she replied. "It's been a tough day for us all. You should eat."

Pushing the beautiful fare around her plate, she wondered if she would have the strength to hold down food. She felt a vibration in her pocket and rush of adrenaline hit her. Maybe it was Dru!

Pulling out her phone, she let out a sigh as an American number popped up on her screen. It would be her someone from her extended family. There seemed to be a new one calling her every month. Hitting the answer button, she held the device up to her ear.

"Hi, Nicci speaking." Her voice sounded hollow.

"Cousin Nicci," a smooth, rich American voice replied.

"Hey, Jakob." She looked down briefly at the screen again. "Hey, why are you not ringing from your normal number?"

"I broke my phone. Long story. I'm in L.A., actually, catching the next flight over to you."

Nicci sat upright. "Why's that?"

"Our pack has..." He paused, and she could hear the sound of flights being called out in the background. "Informants...who mentioned that you might be in need of assistance."

He seemed to struggle with the word. She felt a cold tremor along her spine.

"You're spying on me?"

"Ah, come on now, Nicci. Spying is a bit of a harsh word," Jakob interjected. "Looking out for you is what we like to call it."

"Spying," she repeated, feeling churlish.

"Well, call it what you will, but your father wants us there, so that's where we are going to be. Our flight from here leaves in about half an hour, so we should be there in about fourteen hours, and we have a chartered plane to bring us straight to you from there. So let's say, sometime around late tomorrow afternoon your time, we should be landing. If you could sort out some kind of sleeping arrangement for the ten of us, that would be great. I reckon we are all going to be mighty worn out by then."

"Ten?" Why so many? What did they know that she didn't?

"You'll get to meet some more cousins and a couple of our friends. Hope you don't mind the intrusion."

"No, I guess not," she grumped, but she actually kind of did. They really hadn't asked, since they were already on their way and had made plans before even ringing her. She took a deep breath. This was what family did though, right? It was just so weird. She'd never had anyone looking out for her before, and now she had people flying across the world to protect her. Strange.

"Oh, there's our flight being called for the last time. Okay, well see you soon. Stay safe and lie low. We're coming."

She listened for him to hang up, and wondered again what he knew that she didn't. Frowning, she put the phone back in her pocket.

"Bad news?" Gloria asked, next to her, taking a mouthful of food.

"Not exactly, I guess." Nicci looked up as Sebastian strode over and squeezed himself onto the log beside her.

"What's up?" he asked, taking a massive mouthful of food and shovelling it in.

"Just my cousin," she replied, pushing her own food around again.

"I didn't know you had family." He caught her gaze for a moment.

"Yeah," she sighed loudly. "Turns out I have a lot of family."

"Well, that's pretty cool." He was smiling as he had another mouthful. "Some days, I wish I still spoke with mine."

Nicci saw the flash of pain across his face.

"Of course, they are all brutal narcissistic arseholes, so...probably for the best." He turned and gave her a small wink, but she knew that he was trying to make light of his own suffering. He had been disowned after his incarceration, although technically, the sentence itself was due to his breeding. He'd been charged with serious bodily assault after he was unable to control his bear-self in an argument. His kin preferred to keep their accidents off the record books.

"So what are they like? What pack are you actually from?"

All their years knowing each other, Sebastian and Nicci had never really talked about family, because it was the one thing that neither of them had. It seemed strange to be discussing it with him now.

"American." She finally took a mouthful of food and chewed it slowly.

"Really?" His interest picked up. "I mean, obviously, mine are too, originally. What's their name? Maybe I know them?"

"Knute. Have you heard of them?" she asked.

His fork clattered to the plate and he turned to look down at her, a deep frown on his brow. "Are you fucking joking? Holy fuck, Nicci! You have to get out of here."

#

CHAPTER TWELVE

"I can't." His mother's voice wobbled, and her bottom lip trembled.

"You have to," he replied quietly. "Go get Michael."

"But darling…" She tried to pat his arm but he pulled away.

"Go get Michael, Mum." Dru's voice was firm. With the help from his were-panther healing, and the additional medication provided by his father's specialist were-medical team, he was healing faster than any human would have, but the stitches were still largely holding him together. The only way he was going to be able to escape this place was if his brother helped.

His father was a brutal man, but he also was cunning. Dru knew that the guards would have been told to watch his mother as well. Her caring for her son made her vulnerable, but it also meant Dru could use it in his favour, and Dru was counting on that. He and his brother Michael had always been close growing up, and Mike had taken a beating, more than once, on his behalf. It was his turn to repay the favour, in a very different way.

Her eyes darted behind them, and he knew she was looking for the guards. Reluctantly, she nodded, taking a step towards the door.

Dru whispered out to her, "Whatever happens next, Mum, don't come back here. Promise?"

Her frightened eyes turned back to him and she gave him a small nod, but didn't say a word. As she disappeared, he sank back into his bed. He needed to get ready to fight, but it was hard to muster even enough energy to sit upright.

As he swung his legs around to the floor, he felt another sway of nausea and light-headedness, but righted himself by grabbing the drip-line stand. Pulling open a couple of drawers he found, as expected, that his mother had carefully prepared some clothes for him for when he was well enough to leave the hospital. Pulling them out, he started putting pants on, having to stop occasionally when the pain got too bad or the room was spinning. God knew how he was going to pull off the next step, but he had to try.

Peering around the corner of the door, he noticed his first plan had worked. One of the guards had followed his mother, and there was only one remaining guard at the door. Heading in their direction was a nurse, carrying a tray of fresh food. Perfect, he thought to himself. Sitting back down on the bed, he pulled the sheets back up, covering his jean-clad legs.

She was a pretty little thing, with short blond hair and a wide mouth, and had he been in different place in life, she might have appealed to him. He could smell that she was were, but wasn't sure what kind. But he saw her only as a means to an end. She smiled shyly at him as she entered.

"Hello, Mr Maxwell, lovely to see you awake again. How are you feeling?" She placed the food on the tray and brought it closer to his bed.

"Good, thanks." He gave her one of his best smiles, and saw the slight blush on her cheeks. "What's your name, then?"

"Sally," she replied, frowning as she saw the drips lying discarded from the stand. "You shouldn't have taken those out, Mr Maxwell. They help you to heal faster."

"Oh, Sally," he deepened his voice. "I'm healing just fine. Look!" He raised an arm and flexed a biceps giving her a wink.

She smiled shyly back at him. "But I do have one problem, Sally." He tried to give her his best puppy-dog eyes.

"What is it?" She paused, looking at him with concern.

"I have a big social event I am supposed to be attending tonight. It's a fundraiser for sick kids." It was his turn to pause, and he watched her chew nervously at her lower lip. "But being stuck in here means the kids won't get their money. Which seems a shame, don't you think, Sally?"

"Well..." She reached over and poured some water from a carafe into his glass. "You really aren't ready to leave yet, sir. Your father was quite insistent with the doctors that you needed to stay for a few days, and he's put protection for you on the door."

"That's the thing, Sally," he purred. "My father doesn't know about this event. Because I'm sure that if he did, he would want to me go. After all, sick kids, Sally! They deserve it! Imagine all those little boys who dream about being a race car driver, and how disappointed they will be if I don't show up. And look at me, I'm as good as gold. I'd just need your help to get downstairs. Avoid the bodyguards, media and fans and all that." He leaned in and ran his hand along her arm, and felt her tremble under his touch. "I would be eternally grateful."

She looked down at him, her mouth slightly open before her tongue darted out and ran across her lips.

"It would be our little secret," he added, feeling her leaning towards him. "Just the two of us."

Looking back at the door, she turned and whispered to him. "What about the guard? Why can't he help you?"

"He's one of my father's goons, Sally. He doesn't understand the importance of this like you and I do." He smiled at her, reaching over to stroke her arm again. She leaned closer and he could sense her trembling. He wondered if he should kiss her, or if it would make it harder to get her do what he needed.

"Well, I suppose I could distract him for you," she murmured.

"Of course you can." He moved his fingers along her arm again. "Because you're amazing. But then how do I get out of here? Is there security in the building?"

Her eyes were glued to his lips as he spoke.

"You can take my pass," she replied, pulling the clipped swipe card off her chest and getting keys from out of her pocket as if she were hypnotised. "We're on the fifth floor, but if you take the elevator to the basement you can take my car. It's the red Toyota in park 24."

He lifted a finger and ran it across her lips, feeling her whole body shudder as he did it. There was a time he would have kept going with this. Being who he was, and having the alpha powers that radiated off him, meant that woman were often just hapless victims to him. But there was no longer any other woman in the world for him apart from Nicci. Hers were the only lips he ever wanted to kiss, her skin the only thing he ever wanted to run his hands across. Still, as Sally trembled before him, he felt a mixture of sadness and guilt that he had to lead her on so. But it was better that than a fight that he didn't have the strength for.

"Okay, Sally." He smiled. "I will get your car back to you, and thank you. I will give your name personally to the hospital board for recommendation. Now if you can please distract the guard?"

She blushed. He swung his legs from behind the sheet and for the briefest of moments, he felt her surprise. She pulled, so he leaned closer and licked his lips.

"Okay." She sighed, and headed back to the door, carrying the full tray.

As his feet hit the floor, he heard the commotion.

"So sorry!"

"Aww, for fuck's sake, lady! I'm bloody covered!"

"Come with me. I'll clean you up."

There was a pause. "Don't worry about him, he's fast asleep."

More silence. Peering around the door, Dru realised the area was clear. Walking as fast as he could, he made it to the elevator and pushed the buttons repeatedly. Several nurses had noticed him, and looked up from their tasks.

"Mr Maxwell?" One started to head towards him just as the doors slid open. Climbing in, he quickly hit the close door button and prayed that it would shut before she got there.

It did, but the adrenaline was still running in his veins as the elevator dropped floors. He hoped that nobody tried to get in. Luckily, he made it to the bottom without interruption and as he stepped out into the cold, dim basement he looked around for the right car. There it was. Park 24.

Rushing, he pushed the unlock button on the fob, wrangled the door and climbed in, almost screaming in agony in the process. It was a small Toyota hatchback, hard to sit in such a small space without popping the stitches, but at least it was an automatic so he didn't have the added stress of having to change gears. Turning over the engine, he was grateful to see a full tank of gas. With a little bit of luck, he might just make it back to Nowhere in time. He had to try.

#

CHAPTER THIRTEEN

"What are you talking about?" Nicci arched her eyebrow, her fork paused over her plate. "Why would I need to get out of here?"

"Don't you know who those people are?" Sebastian seemed incredulous.

Gloria, who until that moment had been sitting quietly next to them, intervened. "They're not as bad as the stories say. Jakob seemed to be quite a nice young man."

"Wait, what stories?" Nicci swivelled in her spot to face Gloria. "What do they say about the Knutes, exactly, Gloria?"

Gloria blushed, and took another mouthful of food.

"Well if you won't tell her," Sebastian interrupted, "I will."

She turned again to face him, observing his grim expression. "Your family pack are one of the highest-ranking were-groups in the world."

Well, she thought, that's nothing particularly new. She had already noticed the Nowhere Pack's reaction to her heritage when Jakob had turned up last time.

"They are," he rubbed his chin, "how do I put this...brutal."

Things in shifter world often seemed to involve that word, she mused.

"Well, that's nothing newsworthy," Nicci replied haughtily. "Look at Dru's dad."

"He's like a fucking kitten compared to Preston Knute." Sebastian sighed. "And you have to trust me on this one, because for a long time I ran in the same circles as some of the people he influenced."

Nicci swallowed hard. "What do you mean, same circles?"

Sebastian looked down into her eyes. "Preston Knute is the were equivalent of a mafia boss, Nicci. The guy's straight-up dangerous."

"He's my dad," she squeaked. Sebastian grew pale.

"Holy fucking hell," was all he could get out, his fork arrested mid-plate.

Suddenly, a few things made sense to Nicci. Why her dad wouldn't, or maybe couldn't, travel to Australia to see her. His insistence on using the bond to talk to her rather than phoning her like everyone else. The obvious fear from Jakob. How bad was this guy, really?

Gloria tapped Nicci on the arm, startling her and making her break her gaze with Sebastian. "Look, I think I'll head off to see if Mark and kids need anything, love. Don't you listen to all that nasty gossip. Family's family. That Jakob seemed a nice young man, for the short time he visited. And you have us and the handsome Sebastian now here to help protect you. Everything's going to be all right." Standing up from them, Gloria gave them both a soft, knowing smile before she headed in the direction of the dishes.

Nicci hoped she was right, but what kind of protection was she able to give them in return? It sounded like she was only capable of making things more dangerous for everyone concerned.

"Maybe I should leave," Nicci contemplated aloud to Sebastian. "After all, the gang coming and my family coming. It feels like I'm somehow in the centre of all this mess."

Sebastian lowered his voice and leaned closer to her. "If you leave now, they're all dead, Nicci." She felt a tremor run along her body. "There's no way either of those groups are going to let these people go about their lives without you here to protect them."

God, he was right. They would be slaughtered for simply being there when she wasn't. And the killing would just follow her. Every town she lived in would become another target. She would never get to have a normal life, ever. She swallowed hard.

"So what do we do?" She felt his large warm arm wrap around her shoulder and pull her to the side of his chest. She wished Dru was here. He would know.

"The only thing we can do. Fight," Sebastian replied.

She searched for other options and ideas, anything to avoid the inevitable. But as they sat there in silence, musing over their revelations, Nicci knew there was no other solution. Without her help, they were all doomed and she knew it.

Fine. If fighting was the only solution, she was going to need that food after all. She took another hearty mouthful and looked around at the faces and families that surrounded them. She was their Alpha, and they needed her now. She would finish her meal, and then she would make a plan with the pack—and they would prepare for the worst.

***

Lying in bed that night, she couldn't sleep. In the next room were the low snores of the large bear who had squashed himself onto her portable bed. And she knew that outside, wandering the edges of the township, the pack had designated guards who were keeping an eye on the perimeter. But she had that tight feeling under her skin again, that something wasn't right. And she couldn't shake it no matter how hard she tried.

Getting up, she pulled on some running gear and quietly did up the laces. Perhaps a chance to get out and clear her head would help. They might need her to keep an eye out anyway, she mused as she stood up. Through the darkness, she crept outside and to the firepit, which had become the designated meeting point and the key location for guards to liaise.

Getting close, she noticed that Callum, Gloria's son, was there, rubbing his hands in front of the glowing embers. His eyes darted up when he sensed her getting near.

"Oh hey, Nicci." His shoulder relaxed back down. "What are you doing up?"

"Can't sleep," she replied, copying his stance. "How are the others going?"

"Haven't been back in yet, but they aren't due for another twenty minutes. We have contact." He tapped the radio on his belt. "Then we'll swap, and Brad and I will take over. He's just having a nap." Callum pointed to a tent nearby and Nicci nodded.

"Good idea," she agreed. After all, they had no idea when or where this gang were intending on coming from, or what time they'd make their presence known. It made sense to keep rested. Perhaps she should just stop fussing, and do the same?

A crackle came over the radio speaker. "Home base?"

"Come in," Callum replied, pushing down the button and talking into the mouthpiece.

"I think I can hear something..." the caller said, and at the same time she and Callum turned to each other. There were engine sounds. And they were coming—at speed.

Nicci swallowed, and felt the adrenaline hitting her veins.

"Warn the others," she barked at the pale young man. "Now!"

Turning, she ran back to the nearest house and began banging on the front door, "They're here! Get up! Get up!"

People started to emerge. Children wrapped in blankets were bundled into the safety of Nicci's house with a couple of the older teenagers, and told to lock the doors and windows. The plan was to keep the weakest at Nicci's house and for the rest of the pack to defend as best they could from the surrounding houses and area. The township as a whole was too large to save, but perhaps they could manage protecting the people if they pulled the safety zone in close enough. They hoped. Faces, pale and drawn, began to gather what weapons they could find among them while others started stripping and preparing to morph. Sebastian ran out, pulling on a shirt as he went, and walked straight up to Nicci.

"What's happening? Are they here?"

"I think so." She gulped, trying to get a sense from the sound how far off they were. He too paused, nose lifted, before his head sank down.

"Fuck, bikers. Lots of them." His eyes darted around at the scene unfolding. It was dark, but they'd been told to not use torches or lights unless absolutely necessary. As were-panthers, they had very good night vision anyway, and they were hoping to use the element of surprise in their counterattack. From the soft glow of the fire, she could see the flashes of yellow eyes as those who had turned created a safety circle around the perimeter.

"Don't turn just yet," Sebastian warned. "Lure them in to where we are strongest. I'll be right beside you. They won't get you."

She nodded, feeling her nerves twitch and tingle and the ripple of the change trying to push its way forward. *No,* she told herself, *not yet. Wait.*

#

CHAPTER FOURTEEN

Driving the little Toyota felt a world away from the big V8 engines he was used to. As the poor car's wheels screeched from his entering a corner too hard, he longed for something from his former garage. Darkness had fallen, and the light thrown from the headlights was barely enough for him to navigate, yet alone make out the creatures that might be heading his way. But he had to try. His wounds were still healing, but the rough ride was making them worse, not better. Flinching, he threw the car right and felt the back wheels slide again slightly. At this rate, there would be no tyres left. Up ahead, he knew there was the turnoff for Nowhere. If he could just make it in time, before his father's men arrived, he might be able to save them. Nightmarish images of Nicci desperately calling for him burned in his brain and made his foot push harder on the accelerator. *I'm coming, love.* He talked to her, hoping she might be able to hear him. *Hold on, I'm coming.* It was unlikely that she could hear him, as they were not mated, but he didn't stop trying. Through the glow of the headlights, he finally saw the sign. *Nowhere. Population 0.* Only that wasn't true anymore. There was a population now, and he needed to be there to stop the sign from becoming correct once again. Ahead, a lone figure emerged from the dark and stood in the middle of the road. Slamming on the brakes, he jerked the wheel, feeling the slicing pain in his side as he did it. Stars floated in his eyes as the car sputtered and slammed heavy into the side of a tree, the wheel thumping hard against his chest and his head thrusting forward. A scream escaped his lips before the sound echoed into the empty car around him.

***

He awoke to the sound of yelling, and gunfire in the distance. Shaking his head, he felt something warm running down his forehead. Wiping it aside with the back of his hand, he noticed the smear it left there. Pain radiated down one side, and he winced as he tried to pull off the seatbelt, which had pressed hard into his flesh. Hearing a loud growl from outside the car, he yanked hard with trembling hands, snapping the belt He climbed over to the passenger side, farthest from the road, and shoved the door open. Half-climbing, half-falling out of the car, he found himself on his knees on the dirt ground, the smell of petrol emanating from the vehicle. Giving in to the morph, he felt the splitting pain of the transition before he raised himself up onto all four paws and adjusted his vision.

In his cat form, the picture became clearer. The person in the road was a man, wearing an armless denim jacket. With bulging muscles, he stood silent on the road, watching the damaged car, the rifle he carried pointed directly towards the driver's seat. He didn't seem to be aware yet that Dru had climbed out of the car, and instead stood solidly, with his weapon ready. Dru noted a large Harley

Davidson parked menacingly nearby against a tree as he took small, careful steps forward.

Getting as low as his body would allow, he crept around past the damaged front of the car and into the nearby scrub, his gaze focused on the man. When a twig snapped under his foot, the man turned his body slightly, and pointed it in Dru's general direction.

"Anyone out there?" the man called out into the night air.

Fuck. He paused and lifted his nose, trying to get a scent. The wind was in the wrong direction, and he couldn't get anything. Dropping to his belly again, he took another step. The man waved the gun around, and let forward a couple of shots at the car, the sound of the bullets ricocheting through the broken metal with a loud ting. The sound drew another large man, this time in leather, from the bush behind him.

"What happened?" This man was leaner, and had large tattoos across his hands and neck.

"Some fucking idiot crashed his car into a tree." The other one let out a snort.

"Are they dead?" The scrawnier one started walking up to the car, a large baseball bat resting in one hand. This one had fewer concerns about his welfare, the strut showing Dru that he was either stupid, or more reckless. He might be able to use this to his advantage.

"I dunno." He shrugged. "If he's not dead from the crash, he's going to be in a minute. This whole place is going to get torched. They won't even be able to find a fucking tooth by the end of it."

Dru choked down a growl as the leaner man paused. "Did you hear something?"

"Nah, just you shitting your pants about a car crash," the other one taunted. Dru noted that he had stopped moving and was now just training his gun on the vehicle. "Go on. You might as well finish them off. I'm not calling a bloody ambulance."

Watching the man with intent, Dru crept deeper into the undergrowth as the man drew closer. The man was cautious, as if he sensed that Dru was there, but he couldn't see anything. Walking to the driver's side, he kicked open the door and pushed the end of the bat into the gap where Dru had been sitting.

"There's nobody here," he called out, sticking his head in next and looking around. "Looks like they got injured, though. There's blood everywhere."

"Well, look around the bush behind you, then," his friend replied. "Maybe they crawled somewhere."

Turning, the man started shoving aside the lower scrub to see if he could find anyone.

Dru crept closer, low and slow, until the stench of the man was filling his nose. From behind the car, he was protected from the other guy, but he wouldn't have long to take them both out. Wincing, he swallowed down his already sizeable pain and prepared to pounce. As the man pushed forward another twig and it snapped, he leaped forward, his teeth sinking like butter into the man's leg. The guy screamed, the sound piercing, as Dru tugged hard and knocked him to his feet. He released his grasp and then tore at his throat. The snap and gurgle was all he needed to know that the job was done. But in a panic, his friend had begun running in their direction. Gun raised, he took a couple of pop-shots as he went.

"Dan? You okay, mate? What the fuck!"

The guy moved fluidly despite his size. As he got close enough to see Dru standing over the dead body of his friend, teeth bared, he stopped. With a low growl, Dru flew at him, pushing him backwards. He was quick, though, and managed to get the rifle jammed into Dru's mouth. He could taste the warm metal and sharp tang of the gunpowder as he sank his claws into the man's chest. Screams tore from his mouth as he fought to push Dru's weight away. A leg flew up, clipping Dru on the underside and knocking his balance sideways, giving the guy a split second to roll away. But Dru was faster. Ignoring the now-searing pain that was flooding his body, he jumped again, this time finding his mark. Another loud snap and it was done. Dru spat him out, and fell to his side, the pain and effort making him pant heavily. He tried to catch his breath, but he couldn't.

Then, his ears sharpened. He heard it. A scream.

Nicci.

#

CHAPTER FIFTEEN

The pack were surrounded. From the time they had heard the bikes moving into the surrounding township, till then, Nicci had managed to call in as many of the pack as she could into the safety of their central hub of houses and told them to stay put, excluding those who were going to take the periphery. Large men brandishing guns had been circling the town, occasionally firing into buildings, at whim, it appeared. Parents had made all the children lie prone on the floors, their terrified eyes staring up from darkness.

"Just stay low and silent," she warned everyone as a mother wrapped her arms over her two daughters' shoulders, and dropped their heads lower. From outside she could hear the rumble of the motorbikes stopping, and the heavy thump of men's boots on the ground.

"Come out!" someone called, his voice low and gravelly. "We know you're in there."

She brought her finger up to her lips and indicated for Sebastian and a few of the pack to follow her through the back door and outside. Letting the transformation shimmer underneath her skin allowed for her eyes to adjust quicker to the darkness without changing her form. In the forest around them, other pack would already be circling the men, their bodies low to the ground as their soft paws crept forward. But she needed to create a distraction. Giving a side signal, she indicated for the pack members to move into position, before she and Sebastian nodded to each other.

"I'm coming out," she called, feeling the heat of Sebastian's body at her side, the large bulk of him like a solid wall of protection.

Someone chuckled as more boots hit the ground.

"Looks like the little lady's got balls, fellows," a menacing voice replied. As she turned the corner she raised her arms, and got a quick look at the main group. Five men stood, guns pointed directly at her and Sebastian, their bikes leaning on stands behind them.

"Well now, what have we got here?" The owner of the voice cast a torch over in their direction, making her wince from the brightness hitting her pupils. "It looks to me like you've got a bodyguard with you."

"Hold up," another voice joined in. "Is that you, Seb?"

She heard his small movement behind her. "Yup, it's me."

"You cheeky shit!" the voice replied, giving a small chuckle. "You beat us to the prize. Knew we shouldn't have talked to you at that bloody pub. Don't you get any ideas about claiming the loot, though."

Nicci stiffened. She trusted Seb, but hearing his name in such a friendly tone from someone who clearly intended on harming her was confusing. It made her skin crawl. How well did she really know him, after all? As if sensing her fear, Sebastian gave her the tiniest of touches on the back of her arm in reassurance. No, he had a new plan, she told herself, shaking off the doubts. He had to.

"Look, fellas, we don't need to come in heavy on this lot. They're just a bunch of kids and moms. I know Nicci already. She won't cause a fuss." He stepped forward from behind Nicci, and she realised he was now shielding her.

"We got our orders, bro." Another man spoke, this time letting out a loud sigh. "You know the drill."

Sebastian's body moved just a fraction, and she felt him pushing back into her. Whatever he was planning on doing, it was going to happen any second now.

"And you know, I ain't moving," he growled. His body dipped slightly lower as she realised what he was about to let happen. The men raised their weapons to take aim, and the crack of gunfire flew through the air at the same time as Sebastian launched himself forward. For a big man, he moved with surprising speed, and whilst they got a couple of shots off, his fist had reached the face of the first man without him even getting grazed by a single bullet. Their attention now turned to Seb, she moved forwards, allowing the shimmer to take her again before she felt the hard thump of a hand on her shoulder.

"No you don't," a man's voice said close to her ear.

In her focus on Sebastian, she had let all her senses train in one direction, so she hadn't heard him coming from behind. A scream erupted from her lips, causing them all to turn to her. Anger flared in her chest. She had been so careless to let herself be distracted.

With a gun pointed up under her chin, the cold of the metal pressed in hard, she caught the panicked look in Sebastian's eyes.

"Let her go." He raised his hands up, as one of the other men landed a strong punch straight into his stomach. With a groan, Sebastian dropped forward, his eyes not leaving Nicci.

She held back the urge to turn around and hiss at her captor when his breath got warm on her neck.

"She's not going anywhere. Are you, little lady?" he cooed.

Nausea rose, as Sebastian tried to get up and two more men stepped in to start on him with fists and boots. There was the sound of sickening thuds as they hit his flesh, and groans as they made their mark. But out of the corner of her eye she caught a movement. Golden eyes glared out from behind a house, and looked in her direction. Holding in her panic, she nodded, giving them the signal they had all been waiting for. She swallowed hard, because she knew what it would mean. Her choice was ensuring their deaths.

Like shadows appearing from all the corners, the panthers began to pounce. The men, momentarily caught in surprise at the sight of a group of big cats on the hunt, didn't stand a chance. Pushing her body backwards swiftly, she knocked her own assailant off balance before he could shoot, and he stumbled. A panther swooped in and knocked his feet from under him and took him out with a single bite. With loud screams and the crunch of bones and flesh, the pack took effect, going for their vital organs. Up close, their weapons were no match for massive claws and teeth, and Nicci felt nausea as she saw one of them, helpless, try to scream as blood spurted forth from his neck, making his cry for help nothing more than a loud gurgle. With ruthless efficiency, the entire gang were dispatched in a matter of moments.

From the surrounding trees she could hear pack members fighting for their very existence, and knew that they were facing the same terror. Humans never stood a chance against her kind, and it seemed almost ruthless to let them try. Surely there had been another way? Her whole body was shaking as she went over to

Sebastian and helped him off the ground. He was injured but recovering quickly, his gaze darting around at the scene and his arm defensively and protectively going out in front of Nicci's body, shielding him to her back as he had before. She was grateful for his presence and closed her eyes to try and block out the horrible sounds and smells that surrounded them, but it was impossible.

Finally, there was silence. The screams had stopped and a thick, metallic smell hung in the air around them. Slowly, the pack returned and the ones inside the building came out, their faces all drawn and grim. Morphing back, members hugged one another and soothed their children but nobody was crying. Apparently, they had all experienced deaths like this before, even if Nicci hadn't. Everything about the night felt wrong to her. How would Dru have handled this? Had she brought this bloodshed by being a poor Alpha? By not drawing away the danger while she had a chance? She needed to apologise to them. This was all her fault. All of it. Her body still trembling, she tried to catch her breath, and stepping out from behind Sebastian, she raised a hand up to get their attention. "Everyone, I want to..." She paused. A lone panther was running in their direction, its body moving slower than the others, as if it was injured. As it got closer, she realised...

Dru!

#

CHAPTER SIXTEEN

To see her standing there in the dim light, surrounded by the bodies of men and the blood-covered pack members, she looked like an all-powerful goddess. He felt like he could finally breathe again. She was all right! All his worst fears were wrong, and she was standing there, as strong as ever. His father had lost the battle. He wanted to cry, and shout in joy. Instead he ran over to her, pushing past the throng until he could rub his face against her body and feel the heat and familiarity there. Her arms came down and he felt them wrap around his body, as he pushed into her as close as he could. One hand splayed over a wound and he flinched, and she immediately responded.

"You're still injured," she replied in a mortified voice, stepping backwards. "I'm sorry!"

He wasn't. Being near her made everything seem like it was going to be all right. There was nothing he couldn't cope with, no pain he couldn't endure, as long as she was with him. And he knew that at that moment as clearly as if the clouds had parted and sunshine had poured down onto him. She was his everything. A deep purr rumbled in his chest as he looked up at her.

He could see the sheen of tears in her eyes, as she wiped them with the back of her hand. Turning, the crowd looked at him, their eyes wary. He wasn't surprised. The last time they had seen him, he had nearly torn their Beta into shreds. Pangs of guilt hit him, and he lowered his gaze.

"Dru's back, everyone," she announced.

Was that a tremor he heard in her voice? He frowned.

"And I'm sorry, but I need to talk to him." She paused, looking up at Sebastian. "Alone."

The large bear gave a small grimace but also nodded.

Nicci looked down at Dru. "Can we go find somewhere quiet? I think we have things we need to discuss, and I think I need to clear my head for a moment." She looked sad, her lips tight and drawn.

"We'll get this lot cleaned up," Sebastian added, nodding to some of the men to help move the bodies. It seemed as if that damn bear had already made himself at home, but there were no complaints from the pack. Dru hoped he wasn't planning on staying, but they could discuss that later. Right now, he needed Nicci.

They walked together to the edge of the woods, and Dru watched with a growing hunger as she discarded her clothing before transforming, his night vision giving him the best view. It didn't matter what form she took, she was breathtaking. In her cat form, she was small and sleek, her large, dark eyes glowing softly yellow in the moonlight. She gave him a playful tap with her paw and then started to move away, and he followed her with longing and abandon until his injuries began to flare again. Slowing, she noticed his change of pace, and circled back, rubbing her body along his in a glorious warm way that made his skin tingle. Her tongue darted out, and licked a wound on his side. He tried to ignore the joint, flushing rise of pain and desire as its rough, warm softness carefully smoothed away the hurt. He had never made love to another shifter in panther form; in fact, it had never even occurred to him before, but as he caught her scent in the breeze and felt the heat from her body, yearning drove him.

He stopped moving and stared at her, feeling his lust unfurl and grow. She mirrored him, her eyes watchful, and whiskers twitching. But she was the first to break the gaze, lowering her head and body before the shift took her. As she stood up, her naked body sending his brain into overdrive, she kept her gaze on him.

"You could have killed him," she stated. There was no judgement in the words, and he could feel her eyes starting to burn into his soul. Replicating her motion, he morphed and stood before her, prepared to respond.

"I wanted to," he admitted. "I don't know why, even. I had been watching that bear..." The words "that bear" were spat out almost unintentionally, before he could stop himself. "He behaved as if he owned you, I just... I don't know. I guess I lost control. And when Corey attacked me, I wanted to hurt someone. I needed to."

Nicci continued to stare at him, her eyes not wavering from his own. "Corey is your best friend, Dru, and you could've killed him."

"I know." His voice was softer now, the guilt starting to seep in where the desire had ebbed. "I'm sorry."

"And you scared the pack." She was fighting back tears now, and he could see her lips quivering. "You scared me."

"I'm so sorry." He moved forward, lifting his hand up to her face, and he felt her ever so slightly rub her cheek into it. "I'm so very sorry." He moved his body forward, closer, feeling the tingle of her touch along his arm, and down to his chest. His breathing was starting to feel tighter. Her lips parted as she was about to say something else, and he closed the gap between them. The feeling of her mouth on his made his whole body shake. She was soft and warm, and the sweetest thing he had ever tasted. As he pulled her closer to him, he felt her tremble.

"Dru," she moaned, her hands going behind his head and running through his hair, making the ends of the strands feel electrified.

"God, I love you," he replied, his hands moving across her skin, feeling the familiar shapes. He paused to play with a nipple, and felt the shudder her body gave off. His body was getting so hard it felt like he was turning to granite. He smoothed a hand along her back and grabbed her pert, round arse, pulling her in closer to him. It was as if he would never get close enough to her, and the scent of her was surrounding him, making his brain seem foggy.

"We shouldn't," she groaned. "We need to talk."

Talking was out of the question. His brain could barely form an entire sentence. Instead he kissed her again, his tongue darting in and out of the sweetness until she started moaning. Moving his hands along her body, he found the centre between her legs and began to stroke it. She instantly responded, soft growling and purring radiating from her chest. Pushing it further and faster, he could feel the tension building in her body, and felt his own rush forward. He wasn't going to be able to take his time, as much as he wished he could. Lifting her carefully, he placed her down on the ground, brushing aside the debris to make it more comfortable for her. She was squirming under his arms, her hands exploring his chest and moving slowly down until her fingers wrapped around his hardened cock. The light touch brought stars to his eyes as he threw his head back in ecstasy for a moment. But he was determined to bring her pleasure, and pulling away, he brought his tongue down to replace where his fingers had been teasing her. With small circles, he licked and suckled, the sweet taste of her on his lips. She squirmed underneath him, her body writhing, and small sharp breaths coming in waves.

"Please," she begged him. "I need you inside me. Please."

He couldn't deny her anything, ever. And with a restraint that took his whole body to the edge, he slowly moved on top of her and placed himself within. Her body lifted up to meet his, and the electrical feeling of being with her, surrounded in her, a part of her, was almost enough to push him into oblivion. Hearing his own moans, as if his bodily responses were no longer his own, he started their rhythmic dance, her hips lifting and falling to invisible music. He couldn't sense anything around them, just the feeling of her fingers as her sharpened nails clawed out lines of pleasure along his back. Her teeth grazed his neck and he arched into her again, feeling the pace quicken along with his pulse. The tension began to build and he felt his limbs start to stiffen, the movements faster and harder, until finally an explosion like a thousand electrical pulses rushed through his veins. He threw his head back as his body buried itself deep within in her, and the elation of being together united them as one.

His breath finally returning, he looked down at his goddess, her eyes closed, breathing laboured and lips swollen. She was perfection. And when she finally opened her eyes to look up at him, he heard the words he had longed for more than oxygen itself.

"I love you," she whispered, a small tear trickling out of the corner of her eye.

"I love you too," he replied, reaching down to bring his lips once more to hers.

#

CHAPTER SEVENTEEN

The words had slipped from her mouth, but she couldn't have stopped them if she'd tried. This man, whose sea-blue eyes, resembling storm clouds on the water, had captured her heart. Never had she wanted someone in the way she wanted Dru. When he was near her, every part of her body yearned for his touch. She stretched out towards him as if he were the very sun in the sky. He was the golden centre of her universe. It was both a relief, and terrifying, to have voiced it to him. In all her life she had never known love akin to this, and the strength and depth of it made her afraid. Fear of what would happen if he left mingled with the fear of what would happen if he stayed. Would this feeling remain and grow? Or were they like to strips of ignited magnesium, bound to burn with bright ferocity until nothing of them remained? She didn't know. But as she lay basking in the warmth of their afterglow, with the feel of him throughout her, she felt as if nothing else in the world remained.

He moved, sliding off her, and the cold rush that filled her veins at his absence had her yearning to curl back into him. Instead she turned, placing an arm across his torso and nuzzling in, feeling the now soft rise and fall of his chest as his breath slowed their bodies, both slick from their lovemaking.

"So we still have things we need to talk about, Dru," She could feel the rumble of his chest against her cheek. "Like about what happened with Corey. And Sebastian." He stiffened underneath her. Leaning up onto one elbow, she looked down into his face, lovingly capturing each line and freckle.

"We heard he's going to be fine, but what happens now? Can he return? Do you want him to? And what about Ashley? Did you know that he was in love with her?"

Dru startled, pushing up to meet her gaze. "What do you mean?"

"Oh, Dru." She sighed, shaking her head. "How can you be so blind sometimes? Why do you think he reacted the way he did when you hit Ashley?"

"By accident," Dru corrected her, his mouth pulling into a tight line. "Either way, it doesn't matter. She still got hurt."

A frown deepened into his brow. "I really didn't mean to." He let out a large sigh. "And I thought he was upset because of his mother, not her. And then he started that shit about me being like my dad..."

She could see the downward pull of his lips. She paused, and drew in a deep breath. "Well, you are like your dad, in a lot of ways, Dru—"

"What the fuck? No I'm not!" His body grew still and he looked at her, his face contorting.

She wasn't sure if it was panic or anger before he jerked his face away from hers.

He pulled himself to a seated position, wrapping his hands around his knees, his gaze dropping and his shoulders starting to shake ever so slightly.

Carefully sitting up herself, she stared back. She could feel her own body responding. The increase of her heart rate. The soft tremor to her hands. She didn't want to make him angry, but he needed to hear the truth. Her job as Alpha was to lead the pack, and she couldn't do it if he was bringing instability with every decision. "Yes. You are. Take Sebastian, for example."

A small growl emitted from his lips. "Don't start me on him, Nicci," he warned.

She could feel a quiver of anger roll through her, making her body feel sharper. Her alpha instincts were kicking in. She couldn't back down now. She might love him, but she needed to make sure that he was not going to endanger any of the pack. She was doing enough of that herself. A guilty tang hit her chest. She needed him to be better than this. Better than she was. Better than every other man she knew, and at the moment, he wasn't. Sebastian was. "No, I will start on him, Dru. He's my friend, the only one I had for many, many years. And you have behaved appallingly around him."

"I have not!" Dru's fists clenched together and he stood up, looking down at her. "He's the one who has been making cow-eyes at my mate!"

Nicci swallowed hard. Hearing those words made her heart sing, but he was also wrong. Sebastian had never once tried anything with her, and had done nothing at all that would indicate he felt anything for her other than friendship. Had he? She tried to recall all their conversations, but nothing in them seemed to stand out. But did that even matter?

"He is just my friend," she reiterated. "He came here to warn me and offer me protection, which is, I would like think, something you would offer your friends too. Even Ashley. And you don't see me making a big scene out of it."

"But Ashley was my girlfriend! Of course I would protect her! She and I have a past." He spat the words out, and then paused when he saw Nicci's expression.

Her heart had stammered, just for a second, at the ease in which he had jumped to defending Ashley. As if somehow she was still an item that he had ownership on. Did he feel like that about her, too? Was she just another possession for him? Something to be won like a trophy? Fear and doubt dragged unwelcome thoughts into Nicci's head, and she got to her own feet, shaking off the dirt from her body.

"So do Sebastian and I, as friends. Well, obviously this is just something we will have to disagree on." Her fingers were shaking and her voice sounded hoarse.

"Nicci, I..." He reached for her and she pulled away.

"I think you've said enough." Her jaw tightened. "As co-Alpha I would like to have both Corey and Ashley," she swallowed hard, "invited to remain in the pack. And I would also like Sebastian be invited to join. Nowhere is a pack for the mistreated, and he is definitely one of those. And after he defended them all tonight, I don't think there's a pack member out there who wouldn't agree with me."

Like thunderous clouds, Dru's eyes and voice darkened and his head dropped just a fraction of an inch. "He will not be invited, Nicci."

"Yes." She could feel her anger rising up to meet his own. He didn't get to call all the shots. She did too. "He will. And you will be bloody nice about it and welcome him just as you did Ashley."

"But he's not even a panther!" Dru spat out.

"And you're not the only Alpha around here," she growled back, feeling her claws biting into her hands as she clenched her fists. "So if you don't like it, you can bring it to the next meeting. But I am going back right now to give Sebastian, my friend, the good news! And you will not stop me!"

By the end she was shouting, and she knew it. But every cell in her body felt like it was white-hot flame. She had enough of people telling her what to do. Sebastian had defended her and all of the pack that night. His body wore the brunt of the brutality, which they all could have faced if he had not been there. And Dru's response was to what? Send him away? Pat him on the back and then tell him he's not good enough to be in their group? Fuck Dru. She might love him, but she really didn't like him very much sometimes. And she totally understood where Corey was coming from. The elitism that Dru detested in his father was the exact same prejudice he was showing now to Sebastian. And she was damned if she was going to tolerate it.

Letting the anger flow through her, the change was surprisingly effortless. She snarled at Dru and took off back to the township. There was an announcement to make, whether he liked it or not.

#

CHAPTER EIGHTEEN

How had everything turned suddenly from a dream into a nightmare? Anger rolled off him like thunder as he watched her tail disappear into the bush. Fuck.

And she was wrong! He was nothing like his father. Having a bear in the pack wasn't because he was elitist, it's because he was sensible! From everything he had heard about them, they were dangerous and had quick tempers. What happened if he got upset one day and took it out on a member of the pack? Panthers were strong, but few of them could effectively tackle someone with Sebastian's strength and size in full were-form. He doubted even he would be able to do it, though he'd love to give it a try. Fucking bear.

Growling to himself, he started walking back through the bush, not bothering to even morph, and ignoring the cuts to his body and feet as nettles and sharp edges sliced at him. His wound on the side was still roaring with pain, especially after his physical interlude with Nicci, and now with his heart was equally sore from her words. Making his way to a clearing, he found himself down by the far end of the swimming hole. Of course he would end up here, in the same place she had been with that bear. Bending down, he picked up a rock in one hand and went to throw it violently into the water, when a flash of moonlight caught it on the edge and grabbed his attention. Pulling it close, he inspected it and saw there was a something shiny embedded into the side. What was that? He rubbed over it with his thumb. It was smooth. He tried to lift it up towards the moonlight, but there wasn't enough of it to make anything out clearly. He juggled it lightly in one hand, trying to gauge the weight of it, but it didn't seem any heavier or lighter than any other stone.

He decided to keep it. It reminded him of the worry stones that his mother used to get the boys to collect when they went to the beach in his youth. She told old Irish tales of how if you found a perfect, smooth round stone, and you rubbed it in times of trouble, they would help take away your worries. God knows, he had enough of those at the moment. His thumb stroked over his stone's smoothest parts as he returned back to the township, and it seemed to help.

When he arrived at the edge of the town, though, he could see there was a small group already meeting at the fire pit and the flames had been re-stoked. Nicci was smiling, and Sebastian stood beside her, looking down at her in a way that made Dru's teeth grate. It looked like they had made fast work of moving all the bodies, and the bikes were stored neatly next to each other, in between two buildings. Dru could only assume the bodies were inside one of the houses for now. He would have to arrange to have them burned tomorrow, but maybe that was what they were stoking the fires for? He needed to start making plans to ensure the pack was protected. They had managed one brawl without him, but he wouldn't let them down again. He might not know all of his father's plans, but he knew he wasn't a man who would give up easily, so it was unlikely this would be the only attack. His finger rubbing over his treasure, he avoided contact with the others and made his way back to his house, to put on some clothes.

As he flicked on his bedroom light, he looked down at his find. A dirty pale blue stone was embedded deep within the rock, the edge of it making it sparkle. Bringing it closer, he marvelled at the clarity through it, as if it were a large blue uncut diamond lying inside a steel grey case. There was something so strangely familiar about it.

The necklace! His finger paused, his breath catching. It was another stone like the ones from the necklace that Nicci stole! Putting it down on the bed, he pulled on some fresh clothes, wincing as he levered the shirt down over his head. He needed to speak with her, and show her this rock. Maybe the stones from the necklace were from here? But what would the chances of that be? One in a million? It was too much a coincidence. Wasn't it? Could he have been right all along? When they had first found Nowhere he had suspected that they were sitting on a goldmine. Had he been right all along? He needed her to know.

He reached down and picked up the rock and headed outside, not even bothering to put on his shoes. As he made his way to the fire, he ignored that Sebastian's stance changed when he got close and Dru didn't bother with the niceties of greetings. Strolling up to Nicci, he thrust his hand forward.

"Nicci, I found this." He had caught her off guard, her face going from smiling at pack, to frowning at Dru, and now it registered sheer confusion. "Dru, what are you doing?" A frown crossed her face again. "And I think you should know that—"

"I found this," he reiterated, placing his body between Sebastian and her. He didn't want to hear the words come out of her lips. He had already guessed that she had announced Sebastian could be pack. He could tell it from the smug expression on the guy's face.

"Look!" It's like the ones in the necklace."

She reached out and took it, the briefest moments of their skin touching, sending all-too-familiar waves of desire through him. Raising it up towards the fire, she moved it around in her fingers and the shiny edge of it captured the light. Her breath caught.

"It does look like it," she mused, her lips slightly ajar.

Sebastian leaned forward, the bulk of his arm making Dru move sideways, as he reached out and took the stone from Nicci's hand. Dru held back the urge to bite it. He was now pack, and like it or not, Dru had to ignore his anger and behave like a leader, not a fighter. Seb, too, twisted and turned it in the limited light the fire was able to provide.

"I know this type of stone," he muttered, his voice low and dark. "It's a protection gem."

"A what?" Nicci and Dru repeated in unison, both turning to look at him.

"Well, I think technically it's a type of sapphire," he replied, wiping it on the side of his jeans and then looking back at it again in the light. "But witches can infuse them with magic. It makes them a type of ward, if you will."

"Oh for fuck's sake." Dru sighed, snatching the stone off Sebastian and glaring at him. He was taking outright liberties with them all now. "There's no such thing as witches. And there certainly isn't anything magical about this rock. But it might be worth something?"

Sebastian shrugged. "Just telling you what I know."

"And I'm telling you, you're full of shit," Dru snapped back. This guy was either crazy or he was playing an angle that Dru couldn't see yet. Either way, he wasn't taking the bait.

But Nicci seemed mesmerised by it, and her hand snaked forward. "I wonder if it is..." Her eyes were fixed as her fingers took it from Dru and moved it around in the light. She paused, shoving it back into his hand. "Here, hold this."

She took off in the direction of her house, with Sebastian and Dru left standing next to each other at the fireplace. Looking across at him, Dru noticed that he folded his arms back over his chest, his large tattoos splaying out against the muscle. He had the smug expression of ownership back on his face.

"So I guess she did it then," he growled, swallowing down his disgust.

Sebastian arched an eyebrow. "If you mean did she invite me to join the pack, then yes. Yes, she did."

Dru felt his teeth lengthen. "And did you accept?"

Sebastian smiled at him lazily, as if he was enjoying the conversation. "Perhaps. But then, it's impossible to say no to Nicci. About anything, really."

Dru felt his fur shimmering underneath and had to take a couple of deep breaths as Nicci returned. He knew exactly what Sebastian was implying. This guy was playing games, and Dru was struggling to contain the spark within himself.

"Here's the necklace." She brought it forward in one hand and laid it out to display on the other, the firelight sparkling and dancing off it. It was beautiful, he had to admit, but not as beautiful as she was.

"Try it on," Sebastian suggested, reaching out to take it from her. In his hands it looked like a doll's toy, but Nicci turned and lifted her hair, revealing her long, luxurious neck, and Dru's mouth watered. As he leaned in to do it up, Dru pushed him out of the way.

"Here, let me." It was heavier than he remembered, but as his fingers brushed against her soft skin when he closed the clasp, everything started to feel magical.

Stepping back, he let Nicci turn to show them both, and he could not breathe. She was stunning. The gems, lying so carefully against her collarbone, sparkled and glistened as if they were the stars themselves upon her milky skin.

"Do they do anything?" Nicci was looking up hopefully at Dru and Sebastian.

For the briefest of seconds, Dru spotted something. He wasn't sure what to call it. A shimmer? The flickering of light across her face? He couldn't put a finger on it, but one second it was there, and then it was gone.

"Did you see that?" Sebastian asked with an awed tone.

"What?" Nicci replied, her fingers automatically going up touch the stones in the necklace. It flickered again.

"There!" Sebastian pointed at her. He was right. Something did happen. But what the hell was it?

#

CHAPTER NINETEEN

The necklace was warm as it lay against her skin. It felt different than she had imagined when she had found it in the restaurant. There it seemed beautiful, but cold. Now there was a strange combination of heat—and something that she couldn't put her finger on. Almost like a song that she was just catching snippets from, and her mind was trying to piece together the rest of the lyrics.

Looking at the men's faces, she could register their shock. Sebastian's eyes were wide as he tried to touch some invisible line around it. As he got close, the necklace got warmer around her neck, and he gave out a sharp yelp.

"Shit!" His fingers flew backward.

"What the hell?" Dru now leaned forward, carefully extending his fingers until they yanked back abruptly. "Ow!"

Nicci reached up, but she felt nothing but the smooth, cold touch of the gemstones and gold.

"That's weird," Dru said, trying to get closer to have a better view.

"Not really." Sebastian had a big grin on his face. It was one of the few times Nicci had ever seen him with a genuine smile, and she liked it. He seemed, well, happy. "I was right!"

Dru stared across at him with a scowl. "Rubbish. There's no such thing as..." He went to grab the necklace again, this time with this whole hand before he hollered in pain and pulled away. There was a bright red patch in the centre of his palm, which appeared almost blistered. "Fuck, that thing hurts." He frowned at it.

"I think it's a permission thing." Sebastian spoke to Nicci, over Dru's head as he inspected the necklace. "From my limited understanding of witchcraft, they empower it with protection for the wearer, so they get to choose who can touch it and who can't." Nicci felt a quick rush of excitement. "Let's try! I want..."

"No!" Sebastian interrupted. "Don't tell us who you pick. Just choose that person in your head and then we'll both touch it and see what happens."

"She'll pick me, of course." Dru stood upright, casting disdain in Sebastian's direction.

"Fine." Nicci arched her eyebrow. "Let's see if I don't pick you. What happens then?"

His bottom lip thrust forward just a margin, but it made her have to swallow down a grin. It felt nice to be in control, for once.

Dru reluctantly reached forward, this time with just the tips of his fingers, and once again yelped and retreated. Nicci, repeating over and over in her mind the words keep Sebastian safe, waited for his hand. It came forward, at first hesitantly, before he splayed his fingers across the necklace and her throat in a sudden movement, the weight and heat from the gemstones and his hand causing her to gasp. Their eyes met, and he pulled his hand quickly away but not before she saw something flicker in them. What the hell was that?

"See!" Dru said, a smile across his lips. "Told you it wouldn't work!"

"It did, actually." Sebastian's voice sounded a little hoarse as he showed Dru his unscathed palm. "I just got a shock that it had."

A deep scowl instantly replaced the smile and Dru arched an eyebrow at Nicci.

"Did you feel anything?"

She swallowed. She had, but she didn't know what it was, or more importantly what it really meant. "Just his hand." She admitted the partial truth.

Reaching around behind her neck, she had the sudden desire to take the necklace off. They'd had enough fun for one day. Dru went to help her and she pulled away.

"Don't. You might get hurt by accident." Releasing the clasp, she let the weight of the stones fall into her hands before she looked back up at the men. "Well I think I had better put this back in the hiding place. Whatever this thing is, it's clearly worth more than just the cost of the stones in it."

Her mind wandered to the House of Crepes, and she wondered out loud for a moment. "Hey, Sebastian?" she asked, and looked up to find him watching her lips.

"Yeah?"

"Do you remember what kind of party it was that we were working on our last night at the restaurant? I mean I know we were told that it was something to do with the new owners buying the place, but do you remember exactly what they were there for?"

He paused, his eyes getting dragged from her mouth to her eyes.

"No. There were a bunch of people dressed up pretty flash, but it could have been a birthday or engagement. I dunno. Why?"

"Why would this necklace be at our restaurant?" Ideas were mulling in her mind. She didn't recall there being any other shifters on the night, but she hadn't been looking for them, either. The place had been busy and her previous bosses, the were-beaver couple, had been pretty anxious to make everything perfect, so she had been bossed around a lot more than usual. The stress had made her nervous, and she had kept her head down and worked hard to try to keep them happy. Had there been others and she just hadn't noticed?

He shrugged. "The Beavers might have had something to do with it—?"

"What beavers?" Dru interrupted them.

"They owned the restaurant," Nicci replied, looking into his blue eyes and catching his stare. "The one Sebastian and I worked at."

"Were they, I dunno, around mid-fifties? He's kind of short, with a French-sounding name, and she looks constantly grumpy. They drink like a pair of fish?" Dru had gone a little bit pale.

"Yeah." Sebastian turned to look at him. "That would be them. Do you know them?"

"I think my Dad brought that restaurant." He looked down at the ground as if he was trying to piece together a puzzle on the floor. Returning his gaze to Nicci, he went on. "I had a racing fundraiser a couple nights before I escaped here, and there was this Canadian Beaver couple there. I thought it was kind of weird that Dad would have invited them because Dad hated lesser breeds."

Nicci saw Sebastian stiffen, but Dru continued. "They were banging on to me about how good it was that Dad was going to buy their business, and what a great investment it was. I thought they were talking a load of shit, so I didn't pay much attention. But I did wonder why the hell Dad would bother with a restaurant. It didn't seem to be anything like his usual style, but I didn't care enough to ask. My Dad had, as usual, seemed to have everything planned out in total secrecy. They only piece of information I got told when we were introduced was that he had his team assessing the beavers' business, and retrieving a gift from their associates in a couple of days. Lesser shifters often gave donations to the family in return for protection and it seemed unimportant at the time..."

He stopped talking and the three of them exchanged glances.

"Could those associates have been witches?" Nicci choked out.

"Nah." Dru shook his head. "There's no such things as..."

But he couldn't finish the sentence.

"It would make sense." Sebastian shrugged. "I mean, there were enough of them there, but I don't know about you, I certainly didn't smell any other shifters."

"Me neither," Nicci admitted, the idea of it seeming absurd and yet understandable at the same time. "But do they even smell? I mean, they could have been..."

"It's one of the reasons I ended up here." Dru was looking at her with incredulity. "The night of the gift exchange, Dad and I had one of the worst arguments we have ever had. I overheard him talking with my mother about preparations for my wedding, which I knew nothing about, and that this gift would be a part of it. I told him he was getting too involved in my personal life by doing shit like organising gifts for a woman who didn't even exist yet, and he lost the plot and told me that I needed to sort my life out and grow up. We nearly came to blows, but I saw how much it was upsetting my Mum so I took off. I needed to get away from him, and all the bullshit that came with him."

"What would be the chances?" Nicci looked at him. Perhaps they had been destined to meet all along, and meeting in Nowhere was just a coincidence? She could feel the same question ruminating in his mind, too. She wondered what it all meant.

"Well, if I know one thing about my father, he doesn't like leaving things to chance." Dru's lips drew tight.

Nicci swallowed. He was right. There were bigger things at play here.

#

CHAPTER TWENTY

Things were getting weird, Dru admitted to himself. He wasn't the kind of guy who believed in fate, or fortune, but there was something going on that he couldn't explain. His palm, still smarting from trying to touch Nicci's necklace, was taking a longer-than-usual time to heal. Normally, burns just disappeared in a matter of minutes, unless they were really bad, but this one seemed to be lingering. He wondered what else that necklace could do.

"Look, I think we should head to bed." Nicci interrupted his thoughts. "It's been a long night, and Jakob and my cousins are arriving shortly."

His head snapped back up to attention. "What?"

"Yeah, he phoned from L.A. They were coming to help protect us, though I guess we don't really need them anymore." She let out a large yawn. "'Night, boys."

She turned and headed towards her house, and Dru looked across at Sebastian.

"Did you know her cousins were coming?"

He shrugged. "She mentioned it."

Something about the casual way that Sebastian talked about Nicci made his skin itch.

"What else did she mention to you?" he bit out.

Sebastian let out a low laugh. "Chill the fuck out, mate." He slapped a large hand on his shoulder, and Dru felt its weight and force in the process. Was he showing him that he was stronger than him? It felt kind of like it. "I'm off to bed."

He started heading towards Nicci's house, and Dru felt his legs wobble. Surely he wasn't thinking he would be staying in the Alpha's quarters? Who did this guy think he was?

"Hold up." Dru caught up with him. "Where are you staying?" He had a bad feeling about it.

"Nicci's." Sebastian replied as if it was the most obvious thing in the world.

"Oh fuck no, you're not," he growled. This wasn't even a Nicci thing now, there was a pack order here that needed to be obeyed. Nobody, not even a Beta, would stay with an Alpha unless he approved it as well. He might not have all the say, but he had some, and he said no.

Sebastian stopped and turned, his body seeming to grow larger in front of Dru's eyes.

"Look, mate, I tolerate your bullshit because Nicci likes you. But if you start getting in my grill, I'm gonna squash you like a fucking bug." Dru could see that he wasn't joking.

"Oh yeah?" He felt his anger bubbling again. His alpha power responded immediately to the challenge.

Mark's head appeared out of the doorway of the house they were next to, his face pale as he rubbed his eyes.

"Would you two morons keep it down? The kids are trying to

bloody sleep," he called out, turning and retreating back into the house and closing the door behind him.

Sebastian looked down with a smug expression, tipped his hand to his forehead, and kept going until he disappeared inside Nicci's house. Dru felt the growl wrestling in his stomach and he struggled to control his alpha instincts.

It was late, and Mark was right. This was not the time for an argument and there were kids around. A good leader knew when to draw the battle lines, and now was not the time.

He went home and threw off his clothes before climbing into bed. Staring up at the ceiling, he wondered what Nicci was doing. He hoped she was as tired as he was, and wasn't up for doing anything. Grinding his teeth, he tried to keep himself distracted, but sleep seemed to take an eternity to come.

***

Daylight was streaming around the corners of the blinds when he woke, and looking at the clock, he saw it was well past lunchtime already. Sitting up in the bed, he looked down to examine the scars left behind from his recent wounds. If nothing else, he certainly had a permanent memento of Corey. But the pain had reduced to a mere annoyance, and he was once again grateful for the healing abilities of their kind. He wondered how he was doing, and if he and Ashley were doing okay. God knew his father would no doubt be on the warpath after Dru's escape, and after losing the battle with the Nowhere Pack. He only hoped the pack didn't get dragged into the fray.

Getting dressed, he headed outside, his stomach rumbling. The pack were back at work, and the sound of hammers had begun again throughout the township. But their eyes were wary when they caught his, and he felt strangely unwelcome. He tried to shake it off, and went down to the fire pit. Mark was there with some of the boys, their plates laden high with fresh bacon and eggs. Their conversation stopped as Dru got close.

"Morning, everyone." He gave them a nod and pretended to warm his hands over the heat.

Mark looked across his plate at him with a frown.

"I was surprised to hear your voice late last night. Decided to come back, did you?" His red beard was glinting a little in the sun, but it was the flash of teeth that caught Dru's attention.

"Of course," he replied, caught off guard by his tone. Mark was normally a polite man, but this sounded harsh. "I'm the Alpha."

"Yeah, about that..." Mark started to say something but Gloria walked up.

"Morning, Dru." She threw her husband a sideways glance and thrust a plate into Dru's hand. "Glad to see you're looking better today."

Mark took a mouthful of bacon and turned his body away from Dru just enough that it stung. The boys beside him followed suit. Taking his plate with him, he followed Gloria as she bustled back to the dishes area.

"Hey, Gloria." Her saw her glance in his direction, her eyes dropping. "What was that about?"

"What?" She placed her hands in a soapy bucket and pulled out some dishes, which she dried and placed on the table next to her.

"Why's everyone behaving weird around me?"

She paused, as if contemplating how to word something. Taking her hands out of the water, she wiped them on the front of her apron. "Look, Dru." She gazed up at him and he noticed how tired she appeared. Dark circles ringed the undersides of her eyes, and she had a small frown on her brow.

"We have known each other for a long time, right?"

He nodded, feeling the distinct unease seeping into her voice.

"And I know you are a good guy at heart..." She paused, her eyes dropping down again.

"But the pack have decided..." She swallowed hard, as if there was something stuck in her throat before she finished the sentence. "That they don't want you as Alpha anymore."

He could feel his body sway a little, as if she had actually hit him. "What do you mean?"

Her gaze met his. "After what you did to Corey, and the way you behave around Sebastian, who is a perfectly lovely man, by the way," she rushed out, "we all feel it would be better if we had leadership that was more...solid. And less...passionate."

She was picking her words, but they still stung. "So what? I'm not good enough for you now?" His hands were shaking as he placed the plate down on the table, the food untouched. "But I bet my money is still good enough for you all. I paid for this fucking town with every cent that I owned." He could feel the shake of hysteria starting to rise, his body unfurling and reverberating with each grabbed breath. "I found this place, and made plans for it, and brought you all here to save you from disaster, and this is how you repay me?"

He could feel his anger starting to take control, and he didn't know what to do. This was Gloria, his friend and supporter. And she was staring at him with fear in her eyes. She pulled backwards, and pressed her body into the table, her eyes rounded. Dru heard a snarl coming from Mark, and felt the movement as he rushed towards them both.

Clenching his fists, he could feel the sharp cut of claws through the flesh, and felt himself gasping for air. He wasn't going to be able to control it. It was taking over, and there was nothing he could do.

#

Chapter Twenty One

"Breathe, Dru," she whispered into his ear, placing her hand on his arm. He shuddered, his eyes turning to observe her with his pupils fully slitted and top teeth protruding from his lips. "You're okay. You've got this."

Behind her, she could feel the heat radiating off Sebastian, who, upon seeing what was unfolding as they had walked down for food together, had already fully turned and was now standing inches from her back, paws, claws, and all. But it was Dru she was worried about. Gloria, terror etched on her face, was staring at him, her body pushed as far back into the table as she could make it. Mark, who had sensed his mate's distress, had also transformed and was snarling at Dru from the other side. But all Nicci could see, when she looked at him, was the fight he was having with himself. The beast was trying to make its way out and the man was desperate to keep it at bay. It was heartbreaking.

"Come on," she urged him, reaching out to stroke the side of his jaw. For a moment, he pulled back and hissed before leaning into it, his eyes closing. Placing her other hand on his chest, she could feel it thumping, swift and unabated.

Mark's tail swished as Gloria took the opportunity to scoot out from the bench top and hide behind her softly growling husband. With Dru now effectively penned in by Mark and Sebastian, Nicci continued to try and bring him back from the edge.

"You're doing great." She moved her hand very softly against his skin and felt a small shudder. He curled closer to her, his breathing finally starting to slow along with his heart rate. Closing her eyes to the rest of them, she murmured to him, "Come back to me."

Finally she heard him reply, his voice still rough and deep, "Always." Moving backwards, she looked up and saw him staring down at her, as if they were the only two people in the whole universe. Her heart felt tight and she gave him a sad smile.

"Hi. Welcome back."

Distress flooded his face, as it contorted with the enormity of what had happened.

"I nearly lost control." His voice was barely above a whisper. "I could feel my humanity disappearing."

"But you didn't," she said soothingly, reaching up to smooth his golden locks, which were dropping on his forehead.

Behind her, she sensed that Sebastian and Mark had changed back, but she kept herself still and stayed focused on Dru's face. He shuddered, and looked past her shoulder to Mark and Gloria.

"God, I'm so sorry." His voice was in anguish. "I..." His voice broke off and a single tear formed at the corner of one eye.

"It's okay," Gloria replied, but she sounded stilted and didn't move forward, leaving the breadth of her husband between them.

"For fuck's sake, Dru!" Mark was less quiet, his voice dark and angry. Nicci didn't need to see him to know how furious he was. "You almost lost control? You almost fucking killed my wife is what

113

you did! And here I was, supporting you when the others spoke out about your temper. I told them you were not like your father, but from where I'm sitting, the apple didn't fall far!"

Dru shuddered and his head lowered. "I'm really sorry, Mark," he muttered.

Sebastian let out a large sigh. "Come on, everyone, let's give the bloke some space to think." His voice got closer as he stepped up to Nicci's side. "Dru." He paused, looking down at Nicci for a brief second and she could see the compassion there, before he turned back to Dru. "Look, I've been where you are now. Only difference between you and me is this woman standing right here. Without her, you might not have stopped right now. Long ago, when I lost control, I didn't have a Nicci to pull me back, and the result was a prison sentence and a life of regret. Don't end up like me. It's not worth it."

Nicci reached out and touched Sebastian's arm, and he looked down and smiled at her. There was such a kindness to him, hidden beneath that rough hide.

Dru caught their touch, and frowned before shaking his head.

"Yes." His voice was barely audible. "You're right. I need to get some space and get my head together. I think I'll go bush for a couple of days. Try and get some quiet time to myself to work out what I want to do next."

Nicci gulped. It was hard to see him like this, brought down to barely being able to hold any pack rank, let alone an Alpha status.

"That's a good idea." Nicci nodded at him. "But Dru—" She reached out a hand and took hold of his own, making him look into her face. "We need to take you off as Alpha. Just for now. For the good of the pack."

A sad smile crossed his lips and he nodded, his gaze not leaving her face. "I know you're right," he admitted. "But it still hurts."

She smiled back. "I know."

He gave her hand a small squeeze and then turned to the rest of the group. "Again, I'm sorry. But I accept that I am not in the state to be your Alpha. I'll be back in a few days, and I would like to remain a part of the Nowhere Pack. Despite everything, you," his eyes turned back to Nicci, "are my family."

She swallowed down the rising sadness that threatened to swamp her as he let her hand go. As he walked away from the group, she felt Sebastian move beside her.

"He's going to be okay, Nic," he whispered in his low, bear brawl. "You saved his life."

She didn't feel like she had saved it; she felt like she had been the one to witness it all get stripped away. What does a man who has everything do when he hasn't got anything left? There was something unnerving about the thought, and she wanted to go and talk to him. Maybe she should go with him?

Sebastian's hand fell onto her arm as she unwittingly lurched forwards. "No, Nic, he needs to do this alone."

Was she talking aloud now? Or were her thoughts so transparent that everyone could see them no matter how much she tried to hide them? Looking at Sebastian, she went to speak.

"He's right, love." Gloria had stepped forward and taken over. "Leave him be He'll be back before you know it. And..." She turned to look over her shoulder at her husband. "We have enough on the go with the other pack arriving shortly."

Shit, she had forgotten about that. "You're right," she admitted.

Mark was frowning towards Dru's house. "Probably best he's not here for them anyway," he muttered, arching his eyebrow at Nicci. "Last thing we need is a pack war with the Knutes."

#

CHAPTER TWENTY TWO

Wrapping his fingers tighter around the steering wheel with one hand, he felt the adrenaline fill his veins as he swerved into the corner, his other hand naturally falling into place beside him to drop down the gear. It was hard to say how long he had been at the track. It could have been minutes, it could have been hours. All he knew was the stretch of road that lay out in front of him and the feel of the motor underneath, at his total control. Taking another deep breath, he came out into the stretch and pushed his foot down harder, the car bucking in response.

When he'd left Nowhere, he hadn't known his direction; he had just kept his eyes forward and focused on the nothingness that felt like it was consuming him. When he turned into the driveway of the racetrack, he realised his brain had been doing the work for him without his even knowing it. Racing. The one true release that would both distract him and bring him peace. So he had pulled into the yard, located the lock-box key for his garage door, and started preparing one of his vehicles for a run. He was on autopilot, his body moving in such a familiar way that he didn't even have to contemplate how to do it. The checklist complete, he had hit the track, the familiar smell of the fuel still sharp in his nose.

Suddenly, something caught his eye, throwing him off course. Jerking in response, he slammed on the brakes, the car veering off the middle of the track and a plume of smoke radiating from the tyres. Someone had arrived.

As a sleek, black car pulled into the yard not far from the starting post, he tried to catch a glimpse of who it might be. After all, nobody should know that he was here. Which meant that whoever had turned up was not invited. By him at least. As the car stopped and throbbed beneath him, he tried to get a glimpse of the intruder. After all, they would never outrun him in this car if he should need to flee.

A leg protruded before the full form emerged. Corey!

He paused, his foot not hitting the accelerator immediately. Why would he come here after what Dru had done? Surely, he should be in hospital, still tending to his wounds? But there he was, standing tall with his arms across his chest, and staring directly at Dru's car. There was no way he could avoid him. His foot went down and the car shot forward, pushing his weight back into the seat. As he pulled up in front of Corey's car, he was unable to tell from the body language what was going to happen next. Maybe he was here to settle the score? His arms remained folded, his eyes behind mirrored sunglasses. One thing was for sure: he wasn't smiling like usual.

As Dru stepped out of the car, he could feel his heartbeat rising again, almost as if he was facing another tight corner. His hands shook slightly as he walked towards the immobile figure of what he hoped was still his best friend.

"Hey, mate." He broke the silence, watching carefully for signs of a change. The last thing he wanted was another confrontation.

"Dru." Corey's voice sounded cold and distant, not at all like the man he would normally recognise. There were fresh, red scars along his face dragging down his jaw, and Dru could feel himself flinch as he stared at them. "What are you doing back on pack land?"

Damn, he hadn't even considered that bit. The long drive had brought him straight back to his father's territory, and therein he had broken the rules. Again. He dropped his eyes to the ground, and mumbled, "I had to get out and clear my head."

He felt Corey's eyes on him. "Why?"

"I..." He couldn't even bring himself to explain what he had done but he could feel the sting of tears in his eyes. He lifted his gaze.

There was silence between them, as Corey watched him carefully, before he let out a sigh. With the understanding of someone who had known Dru his whole life, Corey gave a grimace. "Fuck, mate. You've made a hell of a mess of everything."

Dru looked up. Corey ran a hand through his hair before placing his sunglasses on his head and for a fraction of a second, his old friend had returned. "What did you do this time?"

He couldn't say it, but his face must have said what his lips were unable to.

Corey frowned. "Was anyone hurt?"

Dru shook his head.

"Thank fuck." Corey stepped forward, and in a gesture that was almost overwhelming, he pulled Dru into a hug.

He could feel himself crying, but it was almost as if he was watching it from a distance, his mind unable to process the level of pain and grief that this stranger was suffering. This broken man, who had lost everything, was no longer who he had been. He had always believed that he was a better man than his father, but even he was beginning to doubt that. A good man wouldn't have hurt his best friend, nor would he nearly have attacked an innocent pack member. It was Corey's stepping back that brought him sharply back into his own body, and in horror, he moved away, wiped his streaming eyes, and caught his breath.

Corey was still frowning, but not from anger, it seemed. He looked genuinely worried about him.

"Sorry about that," he choked out. "It's just been a rough couple of days."

"It's all good," Corey replied. "I get it."

And Dru believed that he did. As he looked at him, he noticed the dark rings under his eyes for the first time. The scars stood out fresh against his pale skin.

"How are you feeling? Did I…" Dru swallowed hard. "Hurt you bad?"

Corey gave him a faint smile. "You wish, princess."

They stopped talking and looked at each other. "So you've gone back to Dad's pack?"

"Not really." Corey let out a sigh. "Well, not officially anyway. He's tolerating me being around as long as I act contrite and stay out of his way. He can't punish me for rescuing one of his pack, and officially she still is. Ashley's worried about leaving, and I think she's right. We'll just bide our time for now."

"How is she?"

"She's fine, I guess. We've…" His cheeks tinged pink. "Been hanging out together."

Dru smiled. "That's a new word for it." gave him a wink and Corey rolled his eyes back.

"Nah, not like that. Just as, friends, you know."

"Shame," Dru replied, and he meant it. Corey was a good bloke, and despite her weaknesses, Ashley deserved someone like him to protect her and make her happy. God knew, he never would have.

"Yeah." Corey let out a large sigh. "But in the meantime, we have to work out what we are going to do about you. Because your dad's on the warpath. You broke the pack rules when you set up Nowhere and he might be more forgiving to his bloodline, but you are definitely in the firing line on this one."

"Just like old times then, ah mate." He reached over and gave Corey a pat on the shoulder. He winced slightly, and nodded.

"Yeah." His lips were tight. "That's what I'm worried about. Old times mean things being done the old ways, and you and I both know how brutal they are. If you thought getting thrashed by me was bad, you wait until your dad unleashes on you."

Dru grimaced. Maybe it was about time they stood toe to toe? Running hadn't solved any of his problems so far, just seemed to make them worse. And god knew, it was overdue.

#

CHAPTER TWENTY THREE

With all the stress of the morning, the buzz of the arriving plane in the distance made Nicci's hackles stand up.

"Hey, Nic." Sebastian looked skyward, his large hand protecting his eyes from the glare. "Do you think it's your family?"

"Looks like it. Let's go say hi." She gave him a nod, and they headed out.

They had built a makeshift airstrip in the months after the township was formed, just on the outskirts of the houses. With very few visitors and even fewer flights, they didn't need to worry too much about noise in the middle of the wilderness. As she followed Sebastian to the strip, she saw that the plane had circled a few times before dropping in and landing. It was a small jet, but far fancier than Roo's normal twin-prop engine. With a sleek, rocket-like design, it was entirely darkened so you couldn't even tell who, if anyone, was inside. As the door swung open, and the airstairs dropped to the ground, she saw a beautiful woman in an aviation outfit standing at the top of the steps. Shaking her hand, Jakob was the first to emerge, squinting as he looked down at Nicci before he gave her a smile.

Despite knowing about his existence for a while now, it still shocked her to think of him as family. Her whole life had been built around the premise that she was on her own, and as the broad-shouldered, square-jawed men stepped off the plane, one after the other, doubts about herself crept back in. What was it that they really wanted from her? To be family? And what did family even do?

"Nicci!" He came over and bundled her into a hug, his broad American accent sounding out of place amongst the vastness of the Australian wilderness. She tried to relax into his embrace, but her body felt stiff and awkward. Behind him, the team he had brought with him were staring at her, their expressions impossible to read, but their jaws were tight.

"Hi Jakob," she finally managed to get out, as she stepped away from him. "Nice to see you again."

Ugh, she sounded like a recorded message.

"Let me introduce you to everyone." He wrapped an arm around her shoulders and turned his back on Sebastian, whom he hadn't even acknowledged. She was glad to see him again, but she wasn't liking this new side to his personality. Why did all the panther men in her life have to be so segregated?

"This here is Tiny." He pointed to the largest of the group, a monstrous man with dark, liquid eyes, and tattoos dripping from beneath his tight T-shirt, along his arms and down to his knuckles. He didn't move, but simply nodded at her in a formal way. "He's my brother."

Nicci struggled to see the exact resemblance, beyond that they both had dark hair and eyes. He certainly didn't appear to have any of Jakob's charm.

"And that's Josh but we call him Knuckles. He's my sister Anthea's husband. That's Rob, my other sister Maria's husband, and last of the immediate family is Tony. He's my sister Brooke's husband."

Of all the men, only Tony gave her a smile and caught her gaze. The rest of them seemed more interested in staring down Sebastian, who had moved closer behind Nicci. She could feel their challenge like an electrical current. "Then there's Ben, the young fellow, and Hugh, Eddie, Rafe, Stu, and Leroy."

They were a mixed bunch. Some blond, some dark, but the smallest of them looked more like a stringy teenager than a full-grown man.

"Hi. W-welcome to Nowhere." Nicci felt like her throat was tight as she stuttered on the words. None of them seemed the least bit interested in being welcomed, but they were very interested in Sebastian. Pulling free from Jakob she stood back and put a hand on Sebastian's arm, feeling the underlying shiver of it under her touch.

"This is my friend Sebastian."

"Welcome," Sebastian managed to growl out.

Jakob, as if noticing him for the first time, arched his eyebrow and took a sniff in the air before he looked down at Nicci. "I didn't think you had shifter bears in Australia?"

"We are rare," Sebastian interrupted, raising his chin. "But we are here."

Jakob paused, as if considering something, before he reached a hand out. "Nice to meet you." Sebastian took it and they shook, but there was a grimace in Jakob's face before he let go. It was fleeting, but Nicci saw it, and she realised that they were not just meeting each other, they had been testing each other's strength. "We have a lot of bear tribes back home. Where is your ancestry from?"

Nicci caught the frown from Sebastian out of the corner of her eye, and decided now was not the time to discuss heritage. It was already a sore spot for him, having had a particularly brutal upbringing, and she doubted that he would want to delve into the particulars with strangers, even if they were Nicci's family.

"There's enough time for that later," Nicci injected. "Let's go grab something to eat. You boys must be starving. I know that Gloria has been hard at work in the kitchen."

With grunts of approval from the small team of men, they walked back momentarily to pick up their gear, which had now been unloaded by the cabin crew and placed carefully near the plane. In an unspoken agreement, they all turned and headed towards the town.

Nicci could feel the heat radiating off Sebastian on one side, and Jakob on the other, as they made their way into the centre of town. Nobody talked or greeted them as they went, but she caught the fleeting glances from the residents and the looks of concern on their faces. The arrival of a strange pack always made cats nervous, but there was something almost menacing about this team. Which, she understood. They were here to help protect, so each one of them, independent of their intimidating size, must have brought some kind of skill set that her father deemed necessary in a pinch. And if the rest of the pack were feeling anything like she was, the sudden increase in power was palpable.

Mark, Gloria, and the kids were at the dining space to meet them. Gloria's normally warm and friendly face looked tight and uncomfortable. Nicci wondered how badly her run-in with Dru had affected her nerves, as she noticed that Mark and their boys took a step in front of her as the men got closer.

Walking up to the table, Nicci lifted the covers off the pots and pans that had been laid out for their arrival before she turned to them.

"If you want to leave your bags and things over there," she pointed to where an unused house was not far from them, "that house has been prepared for your stay. I hope we have enough bedding for you all, but if you need anything let us know and we will source some. And we have plenty of food prepared for you. There's running water in the house, but we prefer to eat together out here in the mornings and the evenings. We find it helps build pack."

Tiny nodded, and she noticed what she thought was the first hint of a smile from him.

"Thank you, Nicci," Jakob replied. "Go on, you lot. Let's get sorted. I'm starving."

Nicci tried to shake off the anxiety that was gnawing away at her as she watched this new pack invade the space of Nowhere. She could feel the undercurrent, the simmering distrust, as her pack members eyed them suspiciously. Sure, they claimed to be there to protect Nowhere, but what would stop them from taking over? With the pack barely formed, and without Dru there to help in her challenge for Alpha, what would stop her family from simply enforcing their own pack laws onto hers, and taking control? What if that was what they had planned all along? Something didn't sit right, and she couldn't get comfortable around it. But she had no choice. They were already there. So whatever happened next, she needed to put on a brave face. Because her pack needed her to be a leader, even if it meant standing up to her own family in the process.

CHAPTER TWENTY FOUR

"I'm going to have to bring you back to your dad," Corey admitted, his gaze dropping to the ground. "At the end of the day this is his turf, and you're on it. He knows you're here so there's no point in me even trying to let you slip away. It would only mean punishment, for all of us."

Dru nodded. Corey was right. He knew his father would be keeping track of people: that was in his nature. Still, his father's first attack had shown that the Nowhere Pack were not as weak as expected. Dru doubted he would rush in to attack them again so soon afterward. He would bide his time, observe, and try to find their weaknesses. In fact, his father was the only remaining danger the pack had, and perhaps it was better this way—because Dru was the pack's weakness. His inability to control himself made him volatile, and his father would surely use that against them.

He would never take over his father as pack leader, but perhaps his dad might let him continue racing. It was, after all, the only place in the world, outside of Nicci's arms, where he felt like he belonged, and he had no way to get back to her. He felt another slice of pain through his chest.

"Okay. Let me put the car away and we can head back to the pack together."

Corey nodded and climbed into his own vehicle, the tinted window again hiding him from view. Dru walked slowly back as he thought about what his father was going to say, and as he turned on the engine and felt the rumble underneath the seat again, the shaking in his hands calmed. But by the time the car was tucked up under its protective sheet, back in the shed, Dru felt the nerves returning. It was going to be bad.

Swallowing, he turned and walked back to Corey, then climbed into the passenger seat.

"Did you want to put your own car away?" he asked, nodding in the direction of Dru's remaining vehicle.

"Nah. Hopefully, I can come back and get it shortly. It'll be fine." He was about to mention that this place was loaded with cameras, when the realisation of it hit him. Of course his dad knew he was here. He had probably watched this whole scene with Corey unfold. His vulnerability had been on full display, and he felt a tremor run through his body. That would be used against him, he was sure of it.

They drove to the pack homestead in silence, but the closer they got, and the more familiar the spaces, the more Dru found his fear increasing. Fleeting memories of punishments for pack members were ingrained in locations. The places where his father had buried bodies or publicly humiliated people were passing by the window like a slide show, and Dru couldn't switch it off. Their faces, warped in pain, were etched in his mind. Some of them had just been kids, caught in breaking rules they didn't even know existed. He wondered if Corey remembered the same thing.

As they pulled into the family driveway, he could already feel his father's presence. Strong Alphas radiated power, like a magnetic force field that surrounded their bodies. His own father's force had felt like a suffocating cloth around him his whole life, and there it was yet again: the dragging, heaving mass of expectation that cloaked him.

The house, as usual, was immaculate. The lawns were carefully manicured, and the lumbering hulk of the rest of it was freshly cleaned, painted, and prepared for the world like a polished trophy.

Following Corey to the front door, he wasn't at all surprised when it opened automatically, and the carefully presented face of his smiling mother greeted them. Even here, in the supposed comfort of her own home, she always made sure that she kept up appearances. But Dru saw the dark circles and heavy makeup to hide the bruises, and from the looks of it there were fresh ones. He grimaced, and wondered if they were because of him escaping the hospital? God, he hated that man. But at that exact moment he hated himself more, for knowing what might happen, and still doing it.

"Hello, love." She ushered him through the door and into the kitchen without asking how he was. She already knew that answer.

The space was bright white, and every surface shone and gleamed with polish. There wasn't a single line out of place, and for anyone who didn't know his mother, they would think it was perhaps strangely sterile. For Dru, this room had always been their safe space. His father, beyond coming in to claim food, rarely entered here. And there were small touches of defiance at every corner, if one looked hard enough. The small pot of greenery by the window, even though his father had insisted that plants should only be outside. And the handmade hand-towel with intricate birds and flowers woven into the edge, that his mother had made whilst waiting for the kettle to boil for the family breakfast. He would often sneak in early in the morning just to watch as her hands moved, soft and methodically over the cloth.

She moved automatically to the jug and flicked the switch, and he saw her hand move out towards the towel as if somehow she was hardwired to do it now. But her fingers snaked back before they made contact. Turning, she looked at him, and he saw the thin line of her lips.

"Dru, you know I love you, but you have made your father very angry."

He didn't doubt that for a second.

"What happened at the hospital?" Her voice grew quiet and her eyes darted around as if looking for someone. "I shouldn't have left you there alone. That poor girl." She shook her head sadly.

Dru felt his chest constrict. "The nurse?"

It made sense that the nurse would bear the brunt of his father's brutality. For his father, she would have been nothing more than an underling who defied him. The jug started to simmer. She nodded and a calm pushed over her face making, her appear almost as if she wasn't human. "At least it was quick." Like his mother's voice. Fast. Quiet. Deathly.

He swallowed, realisation seeping into his veins that in reality he had killed that nurse. Like his mum, he had known that there would be retribution, and he had still done it. Another innocent person who had lost their life for no reason. Another death on his hands.

No.

He took a deep breath. This was his father's fault. Dru hadn't killed her. It wasn't his edict that had taken her life, or his claws that had torn her flesh. His hatred grew and spread through his chest, making his skin feel tight and uncomfortable, as if he were trying to burst free from it.

"So how is everyone?" Dru needed to change the topic to anything other than what he was feeling right at that moment. To get his mind away from that nurse's smiling face as she looked at him. To dull the ache and anger that threatened to swallow him whole.

"Good. Your brother is going to marry. Did Corey tell you?" There was a strange pitch to her tone, and she was avoiding his gaze, her hands instead moving methodically over the mugs and placing sachets in carefully. She pulled open the drawer, extracting a spoon, and gave each a quick twirl. "She seems a very nice girl. Quite pretty, really."

Her eyes finally met his own, and there was something there. Fear? Sadness? He couldn't make it out. "Her name's Amy." She offered him the mug and he noted the soft shake of her hand as the milky contents swirled.

He took a sip, and there was a sweetness there. "Yeah, Ashley had mentioned something about it. This is nice, Mum. Is it a new tea?"

Her gaze went back to her own cup, her fingers wrapping around it as she brought it to her lips. "Yes, just got it the other day actually. Drink up, darling."

They sat in silence and Dru looked out the window into the back yard. In all the years he had lived at this house, the view had always been identical, except for the changing seasons. As he finished the last drop of the tea, his mother began to talk.

"I just want you to know that I love you very much." She was looking vacantly out through the garden as Dru felt his vision swirl softly on the edges. He went to place the mug on the table, and felt it slip from his fingers and drop to the floor, the sharp sound of it smashing sounding as if it was dulled. He tried to steady himself as the room swayed, and his hand reached out towards his mother. Her gaze had returned to him, but he was finding it hard to focus on her face. Was she crying? He couldn't tell.

"Mum?" he tried to ask, but his lips felt swollen and numb. All that came out was a grunt, and then the room went dark, and he felt his body slump to the ground.

The last thing he heard was footsteps behind his head.

"Good. Get him down to the holding room." His father's voice was low and grave.

Then he blacked out completely.

#

CHAPTER TWENTY FIVE

After settling in, the visitors, rather than taking their time to recover from their long journey as Nicci had assumed they would, instead picked up hammers and tools and began to lend a hand around the town. The locals, who until that point had been avoiding them, now gave them passing nods of respect. As she watched Tiny working on setting a frame on a house next to Sebastian, the two of them almost appeared related. Their large, bunched muscles rippled as they leaned down to heave the heavy beams up into place, then with one hand holding it, they used the other to secure them. The only difference was the tattoos, for whilst Sebastian had a few, particularly around his upper arms and torso, Tiny's body appeared to be completely covered in them. They were intricate drawings of panthers and claws, representations of himself and his pack, she suspected. The dark lines of them shifted like shadows across his tanned body.

"The scenery has somewhat improved around here." Nicci startled as she heard Gloria's voice near her ear. Heat flushed to her face and she turned to give her a small shrug.

"I hadn't noticed," she replied, her hands diving back into the basket at her feet to retrieve another piece of sodden clothing to hang on the line. Gloria let out a small laugh, and reached in to help her.

"Sure you hadn't." She chuckled. "Still..." she paused and looked across at them as she raised a towel to the line. "I think I am glad that they are here, actually, now that I have seen that they are prepared to help out with the pack and things. It will be good to have some protection and extra help."

"I wish we didn't need to have them here, though." Nicci sighed. "If it wasn't for me, they wouldn't even need to be here. It's my fault."

Gloria paused, reached out, and put a hand on Nicci's arm. "Oh love, this isn't your fault. Without you, we might not even have this town. We have a lot to be thankful for and meeting you has been special for all of us. And yes, ideally we wouldn't need protection. But again, without you here, we wouldn't have any beyond what our own pack can muster. We are all very grateful to you."

Nicci couldn't pull the feeling of happiness from her words. She knew that Gloria was right, in a way, but ultimately she also knew if she hadn't stolen from the beavers, there wouldn't be this threat hanging over them. Sighing, she picked up another piece of clothing.

"Thanks. I just wish there was an easier solution than flighting. Maybe I could return the jewels and everything would be forgiven?"

Gloria let out a little snort. "Oh darling girl, this is no more about those jewels than the sky is about being blue. The Alphas of this world would be coming for you regardless of what you had in your backpack. You are an heir, Nicci. A worthwhile prize for any pack. If you had been raised as you should have, your mate would have already been decided long ago. As is it, you're a rarity. A perfect specimen who hasn't been assigned."

"It's not really like that, is it?" Nicci could hear the mortification in her own voice. "I mean, they get to marry for love, surely?"

"Not in your pedigree." Gloria looked at her with sad eyes. "For you, the world is already decided long before your heart gets to choose."

Nicci thought of Dru, and a deep pain settled in her heart. No wonder he seemed so angry about his family. She couldn't imagine not having the right to decide who you were to marry, or even love. Not that she could have stopped her heart from being his, even if she wanted to now. Nibbling on her lower lip, she tried to hold back in the question on the tip of her tongue. But Gloria caught her gaze and gave her a small smile.

"I'm sure Dru is doing just fine, love." She gave her a soft pat on the shoulder. "He won't have gone far. A cat so mad in love that he would contemplate attacking a bear isn't going to be leaving his mate for too long before he comes back and checks on her. We cats are solitary creatures, but our mate bond is as strong as it is for any mutt I have ever met. I just hope he's in a better mood when he returns."

Nicci gave a small chuckle. Mutt. She hadn't actually met a werewolf herself before. Being Australia-based they were rare, but she had met several other breeds more local and native, the main one being the dingos. Known for their cunning and fierce nature, they were also renowned for their loyalty. She always imagined that wolves were like that too. Nicci hoped that in the future, Nowhere would also develop a reputation for loyalty, but she knew they weren't there yet. Building that trust took time and effort, but she was prepared to be patient. Her packmates were worth it.

"I hope so," she murmured, her wandering to where Dru might be and what he might be doing. She was so focused on the memory of Dru, and recalling the minute details about his face and smell, she didn't hear Sebastian until his hand came down on her shoulder. She jumped back.

"Sorry!" He gave her a rueful smile. "Didn't mean to scare you."

Beads of sweat were clinging to his forehead, and he looked down at her face, the enormity of him reminding her again of how easy it was to spot his beast. She wondered if he saw the cat-like features in her?

"No, I was just lost in thought." She gave him a smile. "How can I help?"

"Didn't need anything, we are just taking a break for a bit. We'll finish off that wall before dinner and then tomorrow we can get stuck into the others."

"Well dinner won't be too far off, love." Gloria gave him a big smile. "You boys sure are doing a wonderful job with helping out. We really do appreciate having you around."

Red tinged Sebastian's cheeks and Nicci gave a small chuckle.

"Seb doesn't like compliments, do you, mate?" She gave him a wink and he grinned down at her.

"Depends who is giving them." He winked back and she felt her own cheeks grow hotter in reply.

"Actually, why don't you take some time off with the men, and take them down to the swimming hole? I'm sure they could all do with a cooling off and a bit of a freshen-up."

"Great idea," Sebastian replied. Looking back over his shoulder towards the house where Tiny was finishing off a board, he yelled out, "Do you and the boys want to go for a swim?"

"Does a bear shit in the woods?" Tiny yelled back, and Nicci smiled when she heard Sebastian bark out a laugh. It was nice to see him finally relaxed, and it was the first time she had ever seen him look like he was actually enjoying the company of other shifters.

With a loud whistle from Tiny, suddenly all the men appeared, including Jakob, and walked over to her and Gloria. She was struck again with how quickly and accurately they had responded, as if they were a hive of bees that had been summoned by the queen. She wondered if they had trained for this, or if it came naturally to their pack.

With a quick description of events from Tiny, and some relieved smiles from some of the younger members, they headed en masse towards the swimming hole, leaving Nicci and Gloria to watch them disappearing from behind.

"You should go too," Gloria prompted. "Keep an eye on things, and all that."

"They are grown men," Nicci scoffed. "I'm sure they can manage."

"I'm sure they can too." Gloria smiled and leaned close to her ear. "But I bet it's the best view in town..."

She laughed and Nicci found herself responding with a chuckle before she swallowed hard. Gloria wasn't wrong, but Nicci needed to focus. There were too many distractions walking around, and she had a town to finish. They still had to plan and prepare the defence of the perimeter. And she had no idea when or where the attack might come from, so she barely knew where to even begin. She had spent her life avoiding conflict, and now she was going to have to plan for it. And the one person who she wanted to ask for advice the most, wasn't around anymore to ask.

Nicci just hoped that she was smart and strong enough to protect the pack. Even without Dru's help.

#

CHAPTER TWENTY SIX

When Dru came to, he felt groggy. There were bright white lights peering down at him from the ceiling, and the small bed he was lying on seemed too soft to get comfortable. He tried to roll onto his side, and heard the surface groan slightly under his weight. Blinking against the starkness of the room, he tried to orient himself.

There was a small metal table next to the bed, with a tall glass of water. But the floor was polished concrete, no carpets or mats, and the wall behind it was a hard, white-painted brick. As he tried to focus, he started noticing other things as well. A small camera in the top corner of the room, the red light from it flickering on and off periodically. There was a tiny ensuite bathroom in the corner of the room. Dru tried to sit up, but the room starting swirling and the other half of the room became a mass of floating bars, with darkness beyond. He closed his eyes and held his head. God, it hurt. The strong thumping behind his temples reminded him of hangovers from his youth.

Where was he? And how had he got there? Everything felt strange and foreign, and there was a lingering smell of bleach and disinfectant that stung at his nostrils. Had he been sick? Swinging his legs over the side, he reached out to tried to grab the glass of water that he could just make out, but his fingers wouldn't cooperate and the glass instead went tumbling to the floor, making a loud smashing noise as it hit. He flinched.

From a distance he heard steps and he turned around to notice that someone was approaching the bars that ran along the back wall.

"Hello?" he tried to say, but it came out as nothing more than a messy gurgle. The swirling face of a woman appeared, her hand pausing for a moment on the outside of the gated door, before she finally pushed through and walked up to beside the bed.

"Ashley, where am I?" Dru was confused and his sentences didn't seem to make sense when he said them out loud. Although it was fuzzy and unclear, he recognised her blond hair and the all-too-familiar scent of her.

"Hush now, Dru," she cooed at him, cleaning away the shards of glass from near his feet and placing them carefully on the table. "You're safe. You should be resting."

He shook his head. "No." He blurted out the word with more force than he'd intended. "Where am I?"

Things were starting to become easier as he fought off another wave of nausea.

"You're in holding," Ashley replied, picking up the last piece of glass before she stopped and looked down at him with a frown. "How are you feeling?"

"Awful," Dru admitted. "Did I go out drinking again or something? What day is it?"

Holding had been built even before his father's time, and was best described as a cell block underneath the main house of the pack. It was used periodically for keeping members safe, as it was one of the few places regardless of your shift you couldn't escape, and you couldn't damage yourself once you'd been closed in. Young cubs, when they first started turning, would sometimes be brought down there to keep them from hurting themselves or others in those first painful shifts.

Her hand paused midway between his brow and her body, before she extended it again and brushed away tendrils of hair from his face. It was a gesture that reminded him of someone, but he couldn't quite grasp who.

"What's the last thing you remember?" Her face was becoming clearer now, and he could see that her eyes had sharpened. She looked tired, as if she hadn't been sleeping.

"Well." he sat up, swallowing down bile as he adjusted himself on the tiny bed. That was a good question. He couldn't remember much of anything. Hazy ideas and images came to mind, but they seemed disjointed.

"I think I was driving." He could remember the feel of the car beneath his hands and the rumble of it under his seat. "And there was someone there."

"Corey?" Ashley prompted, her eyes staring down into his.

"Yes. Corey." he couldn't picture it, but it felt like that was the right answer. "I must have been training."

"Training for what?" Ashley's eyebrow arched as if she was surprised.

"The race. Haven't I got a big race coming up next month?"

There was something that flashed across her face, but it was so fleeting he couldn't read it. "Yes." she gave him a smile, but the warmth from it didn't reach her eyes. Why was she being so distant from him? Had they argued? "That's right. You have."

Dru reached forward, his hand grabbing hers. Ashley's eyes widened.

"Have we argued or something? Did I do something stupid again?" He could feel the pressure of anxiety gnawing at his chest. Whatever their differences, Ashley always forgave him when he misbehaved, but this time she seemed to be acting strangely. He needed to make things right. He was going to be in enough trouble with his dad anyway, he suspected.

"No, no." she stepped back her hand slipping from him. "You've been unwell. That's all. Nothing serious, we think. It might just take you a while to recover."

"Okay." Dru ran his tongue over his lips. They felt thick and heavy. "Has Dad given you our wedding date yet?"

She paused again, her face going pale before her gaze darted up to the cameras. "Not yet, but look, your Dad will be along shortly, I'm sure. Did you want anything?" Her voice was tight and clipped.

He closed his eyes as another bolt of pain radiated across his temples. Wow, this illness sure was making him feel miserable.

"Just some water, please?" He leaned back into the bed.

"No problem, just rest up. I'll be back with it shortly."

He heard her leave the room but he couldn't bring himself to open his eyes again. Everything in his head seemed to be mushed together. Flickers of memories were sitting at the edges, but he couldn't make them clearer. The last thing he could fully recall was going to a counsellor with Nicci. No wait, who was Nicci? Ashley, he scolded himself. No wonder Ashley was funny with him, he must have been flirting again. Why did he do this to himself? Sighing, he reminded himself for what seemed like the thousandth time, that his role was pack leader. He needed to protect and serve, and that included being faithful to Ashley. No matter what.

#

CHAPTER TWENTY SEVEN

Over dinner that night, the pack remained in high spirits. The men had all enjoyed their swim, and from all accounts, it was the tonic they had needed to get them to completely open up and relax. There were plenty of smiles and laughs around the fireside as the new arrivals regaled an enthralled pack of their adventures in the American wilderness. Nicci caught herself laughing more than once as Jakob talked of life growing up as a cub beside a town full of humans, and how the Knute pack managed to avoid detection from the outside world. And whilst she suspected some of his stories were for the benefit of relaxing the inhabitants of Nowhere, she also recognised that there was an underlying warning in those tales. He had been raised in a pack which co-existed with humans and knew how to work the system to keep pack secrets and protect members from the dangers of those who would be threatened by them. His pack was both lethal and stealthy, and they were now residing right in the heart of her own. She wondered how long it would take until they infiltrated the secrets of the members that now resided in Nowhere and used that information to help control their own narrative. She wished Dru was there. He would have known what was normal etiquette and what was potentially invasive questioning.

"You look deep in thought again." Sebastian had returned with another plate filled to the brim. He smiled as he took a space next to her on the log and watched over the rest of the pack.

"Yeah, seems like you are getting along well with them," she nodded in the direction of Jakob, who was re-enacting how he had caught Tiny in a headlock as a child, much to the amusement of the younger members, who were gazing up at him adoringly.

"Your family seem nice enough," Sebastian noted as he took a large mouthful of food.

"Yeah, they do," Nicci mused. Sebastian swallowed and leaned closer, the gentle waft of his aftershave passing her nostrils as he whispered.

"You still don't trust them huh? Fair enough. You're right to be cautious."

Nicci keep her gaze steady on the antics before she replied, "So you feel it too?"

"The increased power with them around?" His breath was warm on her cheek.

"Yeah." she swallowed, feeling her skin prickle with him so near.

"Makes sense." He paused sitting back for a moment, and having another mouthful. She saw Jakob's smile slide for just a fraction of a second when he caught a glance of the two of them, before he returned to his jovial story.

"I think they are watching me." Nicci felt like it should be a warning for Seb, but she wasn't sure why. After all, nothing they had done to this point would indicate that anything untoward was happening. But there was something. Some kind of intangible niggle that was sitting on her shoulders, and it revolved around the way that the men all looked at her. It was almost as if there was a hunger there, and they were just moments away from licking their lips. It was unnerving.

"I think you're right," Sebastian admitted under his breath. "But then you are the heir and you are unmated. You will naturally bring out Mother Nature."

"Why does that keep being a thing?" She didn't mean it to come out as sharply as it did, but Seb just looked at her and raised an eyebrow.

"Well it is." Sebastian grinned at her. "Hell, any man with blood in his veins would want you. You add a beast into that mix, and well..." He shrugged and she glowered at him.

He held his hands up in mock defence. "Well, it's a thing isn't it? Jeez, sorry for calling you attractive." Heat radiated up into her cheeks and she looked across the other side of the pack, towards Gloria and her kin, who were smiling and chatting with the others.

"I thought you said that you weren't going to have a mate," Nicci reminded him. On one of the very few times when she had managed to get Sebastian to open up about his background when they were working together in the restaurant, he had been very forceful in his wording around packs and mates. His own family had been incredibly brutal growing up, and he had vowed he would never form one of his own.

"When did I say that?" Sebastian scoffed, looking down at her and catching her gaze. His eyes seemed to draw her into them. "I recall saying I would never have a bear pack. But you're not a bear."

The words hung between them as she found that she couldn't form a straight sentence to reply. What was happening with him?

What did he want from her? Weren't they just friends? Why did her body keep betraying her? She felt his hand reach out and touch her arm, making the hairs on it rise.

A soft growl emitted from Jakob's throat as he towered over them both, and the couples either side of them automatically moved back. Nicci had no idea how he'd managed to clear the distance between them that fast, but he had, and he was now staring down at her, his dark eyes almost glowing with an amber hue.

"Get your hand off her." Jakob's voice was low and barely above a whisper, but she felt Sebastian's muscles tense immediately and his head dropped just a fraction. Closing her eyes, she tried to blank out the almost nauseating radiation of power than rolled off both men.

"I'm allowed to touch my pack member." Sebastian's voice matched Jakob's in its tenor and intensity.

"She's my blood," Jakob snapped back. "And therefore she's my pack. You need to back off, bear."

Oh god, it was happening all over again. Nicci swallowed down the desire to stand up and scream at them both. Instead, she took a deep breath and stood from her position, opening her eyes to stare up into Jakob's.

"Actually, you're both wrong," she snarled, feeling her anger growing and noticing that the pack had now turned and was silently staring at them both. "My pack is this one. Nowhere. And they are both my blood and my family. I am not an object to be owned, nor am I a prize to be won. If—" She could feel her voice getting louder and the tension in it building. "If I choose to be mated with someone, then it will be my choice, and mine alone. So you can stop your male display of macho, and sit the fuck down."

There was a long, silent pause, before Gloria let out a barking laugh from the other side of the fire.

"You tell 'em, girlfriend," she called out, making the pack break into a mix of soft laughter and chatter as the awkward silence was broken. The men, eyeballing each other one more time, gave her a small nod before Jakob stalked back to his position with the other men. Nicci noted that not a single one of them seemed to be in the slightest bit amused. As she glowered across at them, though, one by one they each dropped their head in acknowledgment of her position. Swallowing hard, she sat back down and an electric rush of power rolled across her shoulders and down her spine. If nothing else, being Alpha was beginning to have some perks. She just hoped that she would be able to hold them off from fighting long enough for Dru to return, otherwise the Alpha male role might be taken by the time he got back. She could tell already that there were plenty of candidates for the role, between the reaction of Jakob and Sebastian. And she wasn't entirely sure that she would be able to stop a strong Alpha from taking the role if he truly set his mind to it. She knew that she would concede to a challenger rather than let those she loved get injured or hurt in the process of them fighting for it. Either way, she knew that unless Dru turned up shortly, he would be too late.

#

CHAPTER TWENTY EIGHT

He barely slept that night. Visions and faces kept taunting him. They were pack members that he knew, but they seemed to be somewhere strange. Remote. And there was a woman. He would catch a glimpse of her silhouette and he tried to follow her and find her, but things kept getting in the way. Through the shadows and the undergrowth something, or someone, was calling to him but he couldn't seem to escape. And the deeper into the dream he got, the further she eluded him until he woke up, sweat dripping from his forehead and his hand reaching forward for a ghost.

Sitting up, he wiped his brow with the back of his hand and tried to steady himself. It had all seemed so real. He could almost smell her scent, but something was stopping him. Taking a slow, deep breath, he looked around the room. It was dark, but in the holding cells it was always dark unless you activated the lights. He couldn't tell if it was day or night any longer, and his throat seemed dry and sore. Reaching to the table, he pushed the button on the side and the lights flickered on, causing him to shade his eyes from their bright glare.

Swinging his legs over the side of the bed, he managed to stumble his way to the door of the cage, and gave it a push. Locked. Damn. He waved up at the cameras, hoping that someone would notice and let him out, but there was nothing.

"Hey!" he called out down the hall. "Is anyone out there? I need out!"

There was complete silence in reply. "Anyone?"

He heard a movement in the cell next to him and tried to see if he could make out anything, but the cells had been deliberately set up to make it impossible to see beyond the immediate room.

"Hey, you in the room next door." He waited for a reply, but the rustling stopped and everything went silent. "I know you're in there. Can you see anyone? What time is it?"

"I don't know," a very soft woman's voice replied.

Dru was surprised to hear a female. The rooms, whilst technically made for either sex, rarely had the need to protect the women as, unlike the men who become flooded with testosterone when they changed, the females tended to cope better. So whoever she was, she must have been pretty unstable. He pursed his lips.

He leaned against the metal of the bars and felt the cold of them against his skin. It was actually almost relieving. Well, if he couldn't get out of here anytime soon he might as well make the most of it. "What's your name?" he asked, slouching into the side.

"Amy," she replied. Again it was soft. Barely above a whisper.

"What brought you into this place, Amy?" He was getting curious now. She didn't sound like a crazed, shrieking mess, which was what would normally end up down there. In fact, she sounded almost scared.

"I don't know." He heard her shuffle again and the soft rustle of what he suspected were sheets being pulled up. Sheets? How long was she staying down there?

"Are you new to the pack?" He didn't remember a pack member called Amy. But then, his memory seemed to be a bit fuzzy.

"I'm from Hobart." Her voice broke and she gave a small sob.

He frowned. What was a girl from Hobart doing in the holding rooms? He didn't even realise that Tasmania had packs.

"How on earth did you get here, then? Are you okay?"

"I don't know!" There was a wobble in her voice and a sharp defiance in her tone. "One minute I was hunting a rabbit in the hills, the next—"

"Jesus." Dru gave a sharp intake of breath. "You were kidnapped?" His father was known for doing some extremely unethical things, and Dru had seen firsthand how dangerous he could be when he was angry, but kidnapping? Had his father really gone that far? What was it that he was planning? He knew it would be something, because his father never did anything that he didn't think he would benefit from. He could feel his anxiety rising.

"Look, I'm sure there's an explanation." He tried to reassure her but he struggled to think of a reason that would make sense.

She began to cry softly, and he swallowed hard. "Hey now, don't cry. I'm sure you'll get out of here."

"They told me I can't leave until after the wedding." Her sobbing was getting louder. "But I don't want to get married. I just want to go home!"

"Who told you that?" Dru could feel his body beginning to shake. Surely not? Surely his father wouldn't have stooped to kidnap to get a suitable bride for him? Dru knew his father thought Ashley wasn't suitable breeding stock, but he had allowed them to get engaged. Surely he wasn't going to try and intervene now? Without the Alpha status, Ashley could be farmed off to any lowly pack member. She could end up with another horrible man like her father. He shuddered. He needed to protect her!

"The pack leader." Amy gave some loud sniffles. "He said I had to marry his son."

God. Dru felt his body convulse for a second. It was happening. He was going to get forced into a marriage with his girl. Who the hell was she, anyway?

"Why?" he blurted out, unable to stop himself.

"I don't know!" She howled, her sobbing increasing again. He found himself pacing around the room. There had to be a logical reason she was there. After all, his father didn't do anything without a purpose. He just needed to find out what that purpose was. His thoughts turned to Tasmania.

"I didn't know there was a pack in Tasmania," he muttered to himself, but loud enough that she could hear him.

"I don't know what the fuck you are talking about!" Her sobs had given into angry spits. "The last thing I remember, I was hunting for a rabbit in the woods. The next minute I am here, and I look like this..." She stopped and he absorbed what she was saying.

"So wait, you aren't normally a human?" This was getting weirder than a white rabbit in a storybook.

"Of course not!" A feline snarl, low and feral, came from the other cell. It reminded him of a panther's but it had a different timbre. What the heck?

"I'm a tiger, you idiot!" She was snapping her teeth now, apparently having risen from her bed. He could hear her straining at the bars in the front. "And I want out! Get me the fuck out of here!" There were sounds of material being torn as her teeth gnashed. "I want to go home! You can't keep me in here!"

There was a soft hissing sound, and she snarled loudly. Metal clunked as he suspected that she had thrown the bed across the room, showing that she clearly was strong, as the beds were made to be extremely heavy. He doubted he could lift one himself. In his shock, he barely registered the soft thump of her body as it dropped to the ground.

She was a Tasmanian Tiger, his brain screamed at him. He had thought they were extinct. But his father had found another pure-blood cat, and now he was going to make some kind of sick breeding program from them both. He turned to see a small tube extend from the wall, just under the camera. With a hissing sound, a sweet aroma filled the air and he felt the room start to spin. What the hell was happening? His legs gave out and the last thing he recalled was the sound of his body as it hit the concrete floor.

#

CHAPTER TWENTY NINE

They came in the night.

As a precaution, Jakob and the new arrivals had insisted that they move all pack members into a safe zone in various houses around the centre of the town to sleep at night. They had also picked various locations for lookouts, and begun surveillance. Nicci had told them there was no need, that the danger had already been and gone, but Jakob had been insistent. With his pack experience, he convinced her that the first attack might have just been a test. He reminded her that there was still the risk of others coming, some with far more powers than a mere pack of humans. Back in America, they always planned for random attacks, from both magical elements and other shifters. It was how they kept the pack safe. The thought of it sent shivers down Nicci's back. Having experienced firsthand what the necklace had been capable of doing, she didn't want to know what else was out there. After discussing with Gloria before bed, they had all agreed it was better to be safe than sorry.

Nicci awoke to the sound of snarls in the distance, quickly followed by a sharp rapping on her door. Sebastian entered her room, the size of him filling the space and the shadows showing across his muscled torso.

"Nicci, get up." His voice was terse and he flicked on her lights, making her startle. "They're here."

Body shaking, eyes blinking, she got out of bed and pulled open her dresser, yanking out a pair of jeans and a shirt.

Sebastian walked over and placed a hand on her shoulder, making her turn in surprise. "Don't bother with that." He looked down into her eyes. "You will need to shift shortly anyway. They aren't humans."

Her body gave a sharp shudder, and she allowed him to pull her into his chest. It felt warm and safe there, cradled in his arms. He smelled different to Dru. Musky and heady, and without that sweet hint of cinnamon that Dru had. She liked it, but it made her heart flutter in a different way to Dru. Her brain was trying to focus, but it kept noticing the subtle differences.

"You're going to be fine, love. I got you," he murmured and she pulled away.

Thoughts of Dru flooded her veins. God, how she yearned to hear those words from him, and wondered where he was. But she needed to pay attention. There was more than her needs at stake here, she reminded herself. It was time to be Alpha.

"I'm okay." She lifted her chin, and allowed herself a deep breath. "Let me grab the necklace."

He gave her a small nod and stepped back, the heat from his body dissipating and leaving a void, which she didn't want to explore further. She needed to remain focused. As pack leader. it was her job to keep everyone safe.

"Can you please go and wake Gloria and get the kids to the safe zone? I need to go and find Jakob."

"No need," a male voice boomed as Jakob entered the room. His face was dark as he glared at Sebastian. "Go on, bear. Your Alpha gave an order."

Sebastian bristled, and Nicci reached out to touch his arm. "Please, Sebastian. I need your help," she said, trying to soothe him. He looked down, a funny, fleeting look passing before he gave her a nod and pushed past Jakob to leave the room, the added weight in the shove not going unnoticed by Nicci.

"That bloody bear better—" he started to say before Nicci intervened.

"Just back off him, Jakob." She raised her eyes and her chin at him. "Around here I am Alpha, and I said to leave him alone."

There was a pause, as if he was stunned, before his head dropped almost in automaton, and he gave a small nod. "Yes, Alpha."

She felt a thrill of adrenaline hit her. It worked. She was able to throw off Alpha power. Suddenly she could hear soft voices in her head. The men who were fighting, were now echoing inside her mind. If only she had known that she could do this with all the pack earlier, it would have been much easier to handle when the men attacked. It was hard to swallow down the smile that played along her lips, as she realised that it meant she was now a true Alpha. "What's the status?"

Jakob, his eyes almost glazed now as he stared as her, as if she was controlling his very thoughts, responded. "They are circling the perimeter, Alpha, but we have killed a handful. It appears to be a mix of various shifters and mages, so we are trying to break the spells as we find them. But it's hard work. Did you want them all killed, or were you intending on interrogating prisoners? It might give us a clue as to what their desired outcome is."

A shudder rolled across her shoulders. This was a war, and she was the general. While she understood that this meant there would be likely casualties, she couldn't bring herself to give a command.

"What do you think?" she asked, looking into his face.

He paused, and the fog of his previous words seemed to lift. "But you are the Alpha."

"Yes," she agreed. "But around here that doesn't make me the person that knows absolutely everything. I need your expertise. What would you do?"

Jakob frowned. "Did you want to me to call your father for instructions?"

God no, she thought. That was the last thing she wanted. A small part of her knew exactly what that outcome would be, and she couldn't bring herself to massacre everyone. If she closed her eyes and called him, he would tell her himself. Of that, she was sure. Instead, she shook her head.

"No. Secure the perimeter. Bring me a mage. I have questions for them."

And indeed she did, but not only about the attack. As he gave a solemn nod, she felt the rest of the pack, in their various locations, hear her command and give their own replies. It was a strange sort of internal dialogue that she somehow controlled, although she didn't understand exactly how.

When he had left the room, she dug into her drawer and pulled out the necklace. It had an unusual glow about it, as if something had triggered it into working. She lifted it and placed it around her neck, feeling the warm hum of it against her skin. Pulling on the T-shirt and jeans that Sebastian had felt were unnecessary, she raised her hand up to her neck. Whatever this necklace was, it was powerful, and she would use it to help protect herself and the Nowhere Pack. She didn't need to be a panther to do that, and she needed to let her human mind control the situation. The cat in her would kill them all. Taking another deep breath, she went outside and met Sebastian at the door. Looking at her, he glanced at the necklace and gave a nod.

"Good idea," he told her. "You'll be safer that way. Gloria and some of the others have the kids safely secured. What did you want me to do?"

"Just stay by my side for now," she told him, trying to not let her voice waver. "They are bringing me a mage."

Sebastian looked at her, his eyes growing in surprise. "Can you hear them?"

"Sure can," she confirmed, now listening in to the grunts of someone being bundled along the path towards her house, by Tiny and Leroy, in the far distance in her head.

"Right." Sebastian was silent for a moment, his gaze fixed on hers. "Can you hear me too?"

She looked at him, and felt his words of love radiate along the mind line like tiny tendrils etched into the edge of a glass but her heart was listening for someone else's voice.

Before she could reply, a single voice overrode everything and her brain began to spin.

"Who are you?" it asked.

Dru!

#

CHAPTER THIRTY

His head was pounding again as his vision came back, blurred but working. He had been placed on the bed, but he remembered everything. He also remembered dreaming about the woman again. Her voice had called out to him, and he had tried to reply, but she had drifted away again.

Beside him, someone stirred on their chair, making his eyes refocus. His father.

"Hello, Dru." His voice was loud and made him flinch. "I see you are awake again. Good."

He got up from the chair, the sound of it scraping on the concrete making him wince.

"Why have you kidnapped Amy?" Dru dragged out the words, and despite the slight slur, his anger was obvious.

"Yes, I heard that you two were talking. In fact, I think you managed to get more words out of her than I have all week. Still, it proves my point. She's perfectly capable of being human when she wants to. Nothing that Michael won't be able to manage with her. Although I probably should talk to him about the short-term plan for her down here. After all, can't have her wandering off now, can we?"

Dru raised his hand to rub his eyes, trying to shake off the headache. There was something about Michael that was niggling in his mind, but it seemed just out of grasp. "What the hell are you talking about? You can't just kidnap a girl and leave her locked in your basement, Dad. There's bloody rules about that."

"Well, now here's the funny thing, son." Dru could hear the sadistic happiness in his voice without even having to see his face. "It turns out there are a handful of Tasmanian tigers left out there. And even better, they never registered births. Preferred to live in their cat forms, apparently. But, with my scientists and mages, we have a solution to that little problem. We've made it so she can't turn back to her tiger form unless we let her, so she will stay in that state until she's given me some pups, and we can continue our pack purity plans."

"First, I know you're delusional because there are no such thing as mages. Unless you plan on telling me Santa Claus is real as well? And secondly, what kind of sick fucking idea is that?" Dru spat out the words, glaring at his father and trying to ignore the smug expression on his face. "She's not some bloody sheep that you are breeding off to get a better wool count."

"Isn't she?" Dru's father stared down at him. "Because I think that's exactly what she is, Dru. We all are, to some extent. But to keep this pack strong for the future, we need to be planning our bloodlines. And what stronger a line than the formidable Tasmanian Tiger? The fiercest thing ever to exist in Australia."

"If they were that fucking fierce, Dad, they wouldn't have gone extinct!" Dru closed his eyes to stop the room from spinning.

"Well, obviously they aren't extinct, because I have one in the room right next to you. Honestly, Dru, sometimes I wonder if you got all the looks and Michael got all the brains. At least he understands the significance of her bloodline."

"You can't seriously be telling me that Michael is going along with his bullshit." Dru shook his head. His brother was many things, but a monster wasn't one of them.

"Oh, he will." Dru's father paced across the room. "With you bred to Ashley, you will keep the alpha pack genes pure. But Michael? Well, he's kind of the backup heir, really, isn't he? Makes sense that he would get the diversified bloodline. That way we can control the pack better, because when you are Alpha, they will have to do what you tell them, whether they like it or not. Still—" He let out a large sigh. "You haven't been particularly good at that recently, have you?"

"Stop talking about me as if I am some stud that you manage. Look, I told you, Dad, I don't want to be Alpha." Dru could feel the tension, the frustration, building in his chest. This was the same conversation they had every time.

"And I told you that it doesn't matter what you want; you will be Alpha, regardless." There was a distinct snarl in his voice. "And once we get that other lot sorted, you should be a lot clearer on your thoughts on this."

"What other lot?" Dru felt something close to recognition pass fleetingly.

"No need to worry yourself about things at the moment." His father straightened and looked down at Dru. "It will all be sorted. In the meantime, you need to make plans for your wedding. Can't have you getting pups without a ring, can we? Your mother would never allow it."

Dru doubted his mother would have anything to say about it. This was hardly her idea in the first place.

"So are you going to let me out, then?" Dru countered, his head nodding in the direction of the door. "Bit hard to plan a wedding from in here."

His father stared down at him for a moment, as if trying to communicate something, before he straightened back up. "No, it doesn't look like you're ready yet. You'll have to wait."

"Wait for what?" Dru was feeling agitated, sore, and increasingly angry. He didn't understand what game his father was playing at, but he wasn't going to participate. "And what about Amy? What are you going to do with her?"

"All in good time, son," he replied, giving Dru a sickly smile. "I'll send in Ashley with some wedding ideas when she's awake. Hope you're feeling better soon. You have heirs to create."

With a grin, he left the room, locking the door behind him before Dru could even lift himself out of the bed. Dru let out a low growl of frustration after he had gone, but it was too late for him to hear.

"He's your father?" a small voice radiated from the room next door. Dru had almost forgotten about Amy.

"Yeah." Dru sighed, letting himself sink into the bed. "And an arsehole."

There was a pause. "Thanks for trying to get me out." Her voice was soft, and gone were the hysterics of her previous performance.

"Sorry. Doesn't sound like I had any luck."

"Still, thanks just the same." She replied. There was more silence. "What's he like?"

"Who, Dad?" Dru was trying to stop the headache but it was still throbbing.

"No." Her voice was barely audible. "Michael. Is he like your dad?"

"God, no," Dru replied quickly. "My dad is the only monster in our family. Michael is a great guy. Well, at least, I think he is. He's always been one of my best friends growing up."

"That sounds nice." Her voice sounded wispy. "I didn't have any friends growing up. I only ever saw one other tiger, and they tried to kill me."

"Jesus," Dru replied. He paused. "So how many of you are there?"

"Not many, I think. Hard to tell, really. I have seen tracks but I didn't have anyone to ask."

"So what happened to your family? Where's your mum?"

"No idea. I think she left when I was little, but I don't really know. I've always just been on my own."

Dru tried to imagine having to live alone his entire life, and frowned. "That must have been lonely."

"Guess so... I—" She stopped. "I never really thought about it. I have never been in a human body long enough to care, I guess. Anyway, if I got lonely, I could always bite."

"What?" Dru's ears sharpened.

"We can turn people if we bite them. It doesn't last long, and the change will kill them eventually, but for a while we can turn them and breed, if we need to. It's the only way we could survive as a species when the hunters came."

Dru felt his jaw drop. They turned people? Regular humans? The very thought made him feel nauseous again.

"Have you turned anyone?" he couldn't help but ask.

"No." Her voice was soft. "I thought about it once. But I couldn't do it. I only know that we can because the other tiger I met had been turned. During the last stages of the transformation, they lose their minds. It's quite sad, really. But he had lots of useful information about our breed."

Sad? It was mental.

"What else can you do?" Dru was interested now. No wonder his father had wanted to bring them into the pack. No doubt in his father's twisted mind, a breed of were that could turn others would be very useful indeed in times of trouble. It was sickening.

"I dunno, not much really. I can camouflage really well. One time I had a hunter only four feet away from me, and he couldn't see me. So that was quite fun. But most of the time I just spent hiding away and trying to keep from turning into a floor rug."

Dru chuckled. "I see you have a sense of humour, at least."

"I think that's the human side of me, which is quite new, to be honest. I always shied away from being in my human form, but apart from the fact that I am constantly cold and my senses seemed dulled in this form, it's not that bad, really. Although I do wonder why hair seems to grow in strange places. Why just there and not everywhere?"

Dru laughed this time. "That's something you would need to ask whoever made humans, I'm afraid."

She murmured.

"What was that?" he asked her.

"I said, that's if I ever get out of here," she replied with a sigh, and Dru felt a stab of pity in his gut.

"I'll help," Dru decided on the spot. She needed his help, and he needed to help someone. There was something telling him that, a strange voice in his head that he couldn't shake. As if he knew that someone, her maybe, was in serious danger, and he could feel his body warning him to assist.

If only he could get rid of that headache first, maybe his plans would become clearer.

CHAPTER THIRTY ONE

The person that Tiny and Leroy had captured was no more than a slip of a girl. With wide, startled eyes, and long, dark hair, she stared cautiously at Sebastian, her chin jutting forward as they entered, before her eyes fell on the necklace around Nicci's neck, and she gave a small gasp. Tiny pulled back on her arms and she winced.

"Here's one, Alpha." Tiny pushed the girl forward. She stumbled and Nicci caught her. Confusion spread across the young face as her fingers flickered against Nicci's skin.

"You're not like the others," she stated simply, her bright hazel eyes dropping down to the necklace as if entranced. "And that's not yours."

She was right on both counts, but Nicci didn't want to give away too much. She needed to get more information than she provided at this stage.

"I'm Nicci," she told her, helping her to straighten and stand. She put a hand forward to shake as a greeting gesture, but the girl whipped it upwards with an almost frenetic grab and stared down at her palm. There was definitely something odd about the girl, but Nicci felt safe in her presence, although she couldn't exactly explain why. As a finger darted and weaved over the lines in her hand, the girl's eyes grew round and large and then returned to her face. Her head dropped, as if she was acknowledging something that Nicci didn't understand, and she kept her gaze to the floor.

"How may I serve?" she asked.

This girl was more odd than Nicci knew what to do with.

"Um, well, we…I mean I, need information about the attack. Why are you here and what do they want? And who sent you?"

The girl frowned, and raised her eyes. "You mean you don't know?"

Nicci shook her head. The girl's gaze darted across to Sebastian, who had crossed his arms over his chest. She looked back up at Nicci and her eyes glazed over, as if a fog had covered them.

"You will be saved but you will get lost, you will hear but not be seen, you will find that which has been hidden from you. But beware the man who cannot be found."

The young one shook her head as her eyes returned to normal. "Sorry. I did it again, didn't I?" the girl said, barely above a whisper, and her face pale.

Nicci looked down at her as a shudder rolled through her body. What the hell did all that mean? Was it a premonition?

"Did what, exactly? What was that?"

The girl pulled her lips into a tight line. "I think the more pressing issue is the fact that you need to know about the attack. Trust me when I tell you that you and I can discuss this at a later time."

Nicci arched an eyebrow at her, intrigued. "Can you see the future?"

"Alpha, this girl is playing with you." Tiny stepped forward, the bulk of him bringing Nicci's gaze up. "It's just tricks and bullshit. She's trying to stall so that they can get to you quicker. Let's just kill her and be done with it. I can find someone else who is prepared to talk." His voice was low and gravelly, and his patience was clearly wearing thin.

The girl, half of Tiny's size and a quarter of his weight, swivelled on the spot, crouched low, and spat a handful of words at him under her breath. Without saying anything more, Tiny went pale and began to claw at his throat, his enraged eyes narrowing on her. Realising he was losing, he grabbed her by the shoulders and lifted her up, shaking her with such a force that Nicci was worried that she would snap.

"Stop it!" she cried out, using every part of her newly found power to throw it in his direction. It was exhilarating to feel it rush forward and see their instant reactions. Even Leroy, who was several steps behind, flinched as her words hit, and Tiny dropped the girl like a hot iron. Dazed, she stood up again and waved her hand in his direction before Tiny started taking large gulps of air.

"What the fuck was that?" Sebastian, beside her, looked both horrified and confused.

"Fucking mages," Leroy spat out from the back.

The girl was shivering now and turned to look back at Nicci, before once again bowing her head. "I'm so sorry that I had to do that, Your Ladyship. He was going to attack me."

"Well, I don't know about that," Nicci replied, feeling as if she was somehow watching some strange movie unfold. "But there's no need to call me fancy names. Just call me Nicci. What's your name?"

The girls eyes went back to her face, and she frowned before muttering under her breath. "They never ask my name, they just want me to tell them what is going to happen next. You are very different. I will help you." She paused and tilted her head. It reminded Nicci of a small sparrow assessing something. "My name is Willow."

Tiny, whose faculties had now all returned, was glaring at her. "Alpha, let's be done with this one. She's useless. Let Leroy and me go back out and see what we can find."

"I'm not useless!" Willow hissed back at him. "Let me show you. I can help!"

Sebastian reached out and placed his hand on Nicci's arm, bringing her gaze to his face. "Look, I don't know if you want to trust this girl, but Tiny is right. Time is running out and we have pack getting hurt and killed out there. We need to come up with a plan."

Nicci swallowed hard, and nodded. If she closed her eyes she knew she would be able to hear the cries and screams in her head as pack members fought off their attackers, and she wasn't sure how long she could listen to it before it would drive her insane.

"Willow, what are the intentions of this attack? Why are they here and what do they want?"

"They are here to slaughter everyone." Willow shrugged. "Well, everyone except you."

A shudder ran along Nicci's spine. "Why?"

Willow gave her a confused look. "Because you're powerful, of course. You will lead the next great pack and become the mother of..." She paused. "We aren't allowed to give you too much information about your future. It's perilous for everyone and I would be breaching Council rules."

Nicci felt a twinge of frustration. Mother of who, exactly? And who was this "council?" There was so much she didn't understand about this whole situation. But nobody seemed in a rush to fill in the blanks with her. She hated feeling like she was out of the loop, especially when the whole pack was relying on her to make decisions and know what to do.

"Fine," she snapped back. "But how can we stop them? I need to protect my pack."

#

CHAPTER THIRTY TWO

Dru's head was pounding and he couldn't turn off the noise. He just wished that someone would come in and make it stop. Ashley did eventually turn up, but it seemed to take forever for her to arrive. As Dru lay on the bed, he counted the brick lines in the ceiling and tried to block out the sounds that seemed to be swirling in his head. Distant screams and yells, as if people were fighting, radiated in the back of his brain. At one point he sat bolt upright, as a woman's voice yelled "stop it!" in a tone that made his skin shiver. Shaking his head, he tried to ignore it, but there was something, or rather someone, there that he couldn't remove. The clinging call of her voice echoed and stirred in him, and he felt his body harden in automatic response to something he didn't understand. Who was she? And why did she have that effect on him?

He tried closing his eyes and listening for his father, but the sounds simply returned again. The cries and groans. Whoever, or whatever, was happening, it made his skin crawl and his teeth elongate. There was a dual longing to assist, and fear of what was happening, neither of which he could understand.

"Can you hear that?" Dru called out to his cellmate after a particularly loud, piercing scream.

"Hear what?" came Amy's muffled reply. She must have been tucked up in her bed.

"The fighting sounds," Dru replied. "Do you think someone is attacking the pack above us?"

"I wish." Amy groaned as the bed squeaked with her movement. "But I doubt it. I can't hear a thing."

"Yeah, it's okay. You're not officially pack, so I guess that's normal," Dru sat up and stretched. He wished Ashley would hurry up. If they were in danger, he wanted to be able to help. Pacing his room, he was relieved when he finally heard soft footsteps down the hallway.

"Ashley?" he called out before he saw her face. She was pale and drawn, which made Dru's heart beat faster. "Are we under attack?"

She frowned, her hand pausing for a moment on the cage door. "No, why?"

Dru shook his head. "I must be hearing things then. I could have sworn I heard fighting through the pack line."

Ashley's eyes quickly met his own. "What kind of fighting? Who's winning?"

"What?" Dru rubbed his forehead as he tried to block out the noise. "What do you mean who's winning? Is there something I need to know about?"

A flicker went across Ashley's face before a smooth smile replaced it. "No, not at all. You must be having side-effects from your illness. Delusions can be normal during a fever." She clicked the lock and entered, but Dru noticed that she quickly turned and secured the door behind her before he got close.

Raising a wrist up to his forehead, he tried to check if it was warm, but it felt normal to him.

"Here, let me." She reached out with her hand. Dru frowned as he noticed that his skin didn't tingle with desire. Her touch had always had an effect on him, but now, it felt no different than the touch of total stranger. What was going on? "Yes, you're very warm. I will get something to bring the fever down shortly."

She smiled as he reached out and explored the soft skin on her cheek with the side of his thumb. Nope, there was nothing. No spark, no tang in his throat as the desire rose. Nothing.

He frowned.

"Oh don't be a grumpy bear," she teased him, giving him one of her usual coy smiles. "You'll be fine. You're just not feeling very well, so you're to stay in here where we can keep an eye on you and keep you safe."

As she sat down in the chair next to the bed, the one that had previously been inhabited by his father, Dru's mind was racing. Things didn't feel right. There was something missing, and he just couldn't work out what it was. There was something about the word "safe" that didn't ring true. He didn't feel safe. If only he could figure it out.

"Here." Ashley pulled a small notebook out that had been tucked into a pocket and she opened it up. "Your father has told me that he wants us to get married the day after tomorrow."

"Why so soon? What's the sudden rush?" Dru asked, sitting down on the bed next to her.

"It's an auspicious lunar eclipse night." Ashley wouldn't meet Dru's gaze, and he felt his own eyes narrow at her. Something wasn't right. "He said it would bring us luck in our marriage."

Since when had his father ever relied on luck?

"So I have prepared as much as I can without your help because you have been so unwell, but I have a couple of questions. Did you want Corey as your best man?"

There was a flicker of pain in her voice as he said his name.

"Yeah, of course, why? Has something happened to him?"

"No, no, nothing at all." She gave him a smile but it once again didn't reach her eyes.

"Hey, Ashley?" He reached out and placed a hand on her arm, waiting until she stared into his eyes. "We've known each other our whole lives. If there's something you need to tell me, you can. You know that, right?"

Another flicker, but she smiled again.

"Of course, love," she cooed, placing a hand over top of his. "But everything is fine." There was a steeliness to her voice that Dru caught. "Everything is exactly how is it supposed to be."

He fought off the desire to pull his hand away, instead feeling a soft tightening in his stomach. Giving him a final pat, she opened up the book and began to throw questions about colours and arrangements at him while all the time, in the back of his head, something screamed at him that it felt all wrong.

"So I was thinking white and gold, but what do you think?" Ashley looked across at him as he caught the end of her sentence.

"Sorry, what?"

"Andrew Maxwell, would you pay attention please! This is important. As I was saying…"

But he lost the end of the conversation again. There was something in the way she said his name in entirety that triggered something.

"Hey Ash, did we have a fight recently?" he asked her, frowning.

She stopped talking instantly, her face growing just a fraction paler than it had been.

"Not that I can remember," she answered, closing the book quickly.

"Huh." Dru rubbed his eyes and tried to drown out the increasingly pounding headache. "I just thought I remembered something there for a minute."

Ashley sat deathly still, not even breathing for a fleeting moment, before she stood up abruptly from the chair.

"I'm sorry. You must still be feeling unwell, and here I am rabbiting on about plans and stuff. I will let you rest." She paused when she reached the door and glanced up at the cameras. "I'll see if your father will let you move into the guest room tomorrow. That might make you feel better. Anyway, we need you to be rested for the big day."

Dru frowned. "I was kind of hoping to get out of here today, actually," he admitted. "I don't think I'm a danger to anyone."

"Better to be safe than sorry." Ashley turned and smiled at him, and he felt strangely repelled by it. "I'll get your mum to drop by later and bring you some medication. I know she's dying to see you."

"Okay," Dru agreed. "Tell her I need to speak with Michael as well."

Ashley frowned. "Oh I don't know that will be necessary," she replied. "He has his own wedding plans to arrange."

And with that she departed and Dru was left wondering if Michael was feeling as anxious about his pending nuptials as he was.

CHAPTER THIRTY THREE

With Willow's help, Nicci's pack managed to avoid most of the mage traps, but the girl's visions weren't exactly clear, and already they'd had casualties. As Tiny dragged in the shredded body of Hugh and placed him carefully down in the makeshift infirmary, Nicci saw the frown of concern on Clare's face.

"What happened?" she asked Tiny as she rushed to his side, her hands carefully tracing over the red gashes and exposing the wounds.

"Some kind of magic net, I think," Tiny replied, sounding exhausted. He slumped down into a chair next to them. "We have been holding off the worst of the shifters, but those fucking mages..." He swore under his breath, but clamped down his mouth when he saw Willow enter the room.

"What is it?" Nicci asked Willow, who got close to inspect Hugh, who was now completely delirious and writhing in pain.

"An entrapment spell." She frowned. "It is intended to kill everyone except the person it has been designed for." She looked back up at Nicci. "Which would be you."

"Well, is there anything we can do for him?" Clare was pale as she examined his body. "Balms? Stitches? Will anything work?"

Willow shook her head sadly. "No," she admitted. "The best thing you can do is help him with the pain. It won't be long now."

Tiny let out a loud growl and snapped his teeth in her direction.

"Fucking mages!" he cursed, storming out of the room, leaving them alone with the groaning Hugh.

"Do what you can for him, Clare." Nicci felt the tightness in her chest. "I'll go find Tiny and make sure he is all right. Willow, can you please keep working on that protection spell for around the safe zone. I don't want a single child hurt, so make sure it only lets in those who intend no harm to those kids."

Willow nodded and turned to disappear again. Looking down at the writhing body of Hugh, Nicci placed a hand on his arm and for a moment he seemed to pause and sigh, as if she were offering a balm, before the groans took back hold.

Leaving the room and stepping out into the cold, early morning air, she rubbed her fingers across her eyes. It had been a long night, and they were still not done. She had heard the screams and cries of every single wounded or dying pack member, and her head was pounding. Tears pricked at the corners of her eyes, and every bone in her body ached, but she knew that they had to fight on. She also knew, from the reports coming back in to her, that the attackers numbers were dwindling. If they could just hold out a little longer, they would be safe. For now.

She stretched her thoughts to try and locate Tiny, and found herself drawn towards the lake. Starting out on foot, she headed to where she thought he was, her ears pricked as she went. It was a dangerous move to go out alone, but she couldn't bring herself to put others in direct danger again. She could do this, she told herself stoically. Sunlight was glistening on the tops of the trees, a warm red hue hovering above them as her eyes naturally adjusted to the decreasing shadows. The air was still cool but she didn't feel the cold; she was too focused on the movements around her. A twig snapped ahead, and she stopped mid-stride, her body lowering and her eyes and teeth sharpening. A rabbit head popped up from behind a log, and she caught her breath again. Just keep going, she scolded herself. She wished that Sebastian was around, but he had gone off with Jakob to protect the boundary after she had insisted that he was more useful to them than to her. If only Dru was there: he would know what to do. Her body yearned for him, and even though she knew she was in perilous danger, she still wanted nothing more than to run into the scrub land and find him. But he wasn't there. She knew that too.

For a few days she hadn't sensed him, apart from fleeting moments where she thought she could hear his voice. Wherever he was, it wasn't near Nowhere, and she was torn between wanting him there and relief that at least he was safe from the fighting.

Up ahead, she caught the sounds of someone moving through the bush. She dropped down again, her fingers curling around the necklace. It will protect me, she reminded herself. I will be fine. She took another step, the feeling of whiskers starting to protrude from her cheeks as her ears tightened for more sounds. If she turned, the necklace would surely break off in the process. It was made for a slender human neck, not the large furry one she'd have if she turned. Taking a deep breath, she calmed herself and felt the whiskers retreat again. She kept moving, pausing when she heard sounds or saw movement, but maintaining momentum towards the lake.

Finally, the trees opened out and the lake became visible. Tiny, in his full panther form, was pacing along the edge, and when he heard her arrive he swivelled on the spot, his lips curling and his ears flattening before he recognised her. Dipping his head, he invited her towards him, but his body was taut and cautious.

"Tiny," Nicci greeted him, as the massive bulk of his panther form stepped forward to greet her. As a man he was big; as a cat he was a monster. Deep scars ran through his fur, with one tracing down along his neck.

"Jesus, how did you get all those?" Nicci pointed to his body, and he gave a sort of cat shrug. It explained the multiple tattoos he wore in human form. There wasn't a better way to hide them on a body than to make them into a picture. "I just came to check that you are all right. You looked upset back there."

He paused, his eyes examining hers before he dropped low and transformed. It looked more painful for him than most, as if his body didn't like to be in this alternative form. But when he stood up naked, all muscles and tattoos, Nicci almost gasped from it. She knew he had been covered, but scars were everywhere. Like a storybook, his whole being spoke of fighting and loss. She didn't know where to look in order to give him respect, privacy, and felt the heat in her cheeks.

"Sorry." He gave her a small smile. "Sometimes my human form can be a bit much for people. They don't like the artwork."

"No," Nicci reassured him. "It's not that, it's just..." She felt a profound sadness for him, and wanted to reach out and tell him that, but his jaw squared.

"How can I help you, Alpha?" His voice was monotone, as if a soldier was asking commands of his leader. His shoulders squared and his gaze left hers and moved to the ground in a form of submission.

"I was just checking on you," Nicci replied. "You seemed upset."

"No, ma'am," he replied, again with a monotone. "I just needed to check the perimeter. I am doing my duty. Protecting the asset."

"You mean, me?" She arched her eyebrow at him.

"Yes, ma'am."

"Thank you, Tiny," she acknowledged. "I know that you and Hugh were friends."

His jaw tightened but he didn't return his gaze.

"That is the way of battle," Tiny replied, but in a low and quiet voice. They stood in silence for a moment.

That was when she heard it.

The soft growl from within her head. It was deep, and menacing, as if someone were about to pounce, but there was nobody but her and Tiny around. Her body automatically responded with a speed and ferocity she hadn't experienced before. With little pain, but the sharp sounds of clothing shredding and the ping of the necklace breaking free, she found herself standing on all fours, her teeth bared and her hackles raised. But the second it had taken her to realise that her protection was gone was all it took for him to pounce.

CHAPTER THIRTY FOUR

Dru woke up with a startle. Fear. There was someone in trouble. He could feel it running through his body as if someone had poured cold water onto his every nerve ending. Sitting upright, he felt his teeth sharpening. Protect. He needed to protect her. But who? Who was it that was making his heart pound and his throat dry? This woman who plagued his dreams and called to him like a siren? He needed to find her.

Running at the cage doors, he began to frantically pound on them.

"Help!" he cried. "Let me out of here!"

His blood was simmering in his veins as if it was on fire. Unable to control himself, he shifted, the clothing he was wearing shredding from his body, but he didn't feel anything except for the overwhelming desire to protect. He growled in frustration, the sound of it echoing through the cold space.

"Are you okay?" Amy called to him from next cage. "What happened?"

He couldn't respond, his desire to escape so overwhelming that he would have torn the very wall itself to shreds if he had been capable. Then there was the soft hissing sound again. He turned and sharpened his eyes on the small hose protruding from just below the camera. No! He had to escape, he had to...

The room swayed and he felt his legs give way.

Save her. He had to save her.

***

When he awoke the second time, he felt the cold restraints around his ankles and wrists before he even opened his eyes. When he did his vision was blurry, and his headache was back like a throbbing nightmare that wouldn't go away. He groaned and tried to move his arm to rub his eyes but they were stuck fast by his sides. Images, fleeting and terrifying, were raging through his mind but he couldn't get clarity around who they were, or where. In the chair next to him was his father, a deep, dark frown on his face.

"Good morning, Dru." His voice was short and sharp. "Given your behaviour this morning, we thought that shackles might be required. For your own safety, as much as ours."

He stood up, now towering like a titan over Dru in the bed. "But we also felt it might be beneficial to bring proceedings forward. Once you are married and mated, you should quieten down again and stop this nonsense. So your mother will be through shortly with your attire for this afternoon. I have nominated Corey as your best man. And since we are organising the affair, I have arranged for Michael to do it with Amy at the same time. A double wedding, if you will. No point mucking around. You're both old enough now, and god knows I am tired of all the childish behaviour around here. Mated pairs are more settled, and that's what you need. So…" He frowned again at him. "Enough of the dramatics, son. Chin up, and on with it."

Dru felt fuzzy, as if it was all a dream. What? Mated? Tingles of memory tempted him and then disappeared again.

"What's happening?" he muttered, trying to catch his bearings.

His father let out a loud sigh. "Oh, for crying out loud. Just stay there and don't move. Your mother will be in shortly to fix you up. Don't make me have to put you out again."

What the hell was going on? His head hurt. With a click of his tongue, his father set off, out the door, leaving it open this time. But with Dru tied down to the bed, there was little he could do but watch him leave. He heard him pause outside the cage next door.

"And you better get ready too, little miss. And if you hiss at a single person today, I will have you drugged up and brought back down here as quick as you can swipe a paw."

Dru thought he heard her scuttle towards the back of the room, but he couldn't see anything. After his father left, he heard very soft sobs coming from Amy's area.

"You're going to be okay, Amy," he told her, closing his eyes to try and block out the pounding headache. "I promise."

The sobbing subsided but she didn't reply.

Before long, he heard people approaching. He wriggled in his restraints and tried to lift his head to see who it was.

His mother's face appeared beside him. It was drawn tight, and she was very pale. Over one arm was slung a suit on a hanger and in her hands she carried some shiny black shoes.

"Hello, love," she cooed, as he caught the small tear that trickled from the corner of her eye. She gave him a wobbly smile. "It's a big day for you, isn't it!"

"Is it?" Dru replied, his tongue feeling furry and awkward. "What's all this rush for, all of a sudden, Mum? I thought Ashley said we weren't doing it till tomorrow?"

"Well, your father was worried about you and your brother, and he thought that this might help you both get more settled."

"Where is Michael?" Dru asked, trying to swallow but finding his throat parched.

"He's just upstairs, getting ready with Corey. We got you boys matching suits, which will be quite lovely, I'm sure." Dru heard the sound of girls chatting down the hallway.

"That will be the ladies for Amy. One minute, son, I'll come back. I just have to get her started." His mother placed the shoes on the floor and carefully put the suit over the back of the chair. She bustled out the door and out of his view, although he could hear the girls entering and talking softly in the room next door. A howl from Amy was hushed down by his mother, before the footsteps returned.

"All right, love, let's get you up out of there." She leaned down to the restraints on his body and produced a small key, which she used to unlock him. As she did, he pulled his wrists free and began rubbing at where the cuffs had been. When he sat up, the room spun and he felt her hand go to his shoulder.

"Just take your time, love. You've had a lot," she told him.

A lot of what, exactly? Sleep? Illness? Everything about this time seemed to be hazy, as if he was watching it happen to someone else. He couldn't even remember when he'd eaten last. And there was always this nagging sensation in the back of his mind that he was forgetting something. Or someone.

She reached over and gave him the clothes from the chair.

"Why don't you go get changed in the bathroom, and I will stay here for you. Don't be too long. Your father will be waiting."

Dru got up, and felt the aching in his bones. How long had he been down there. Days? Weeks? He couldn't remember. As he took a step forward, the room spun around, and his mother reached out and grabbed his arm.

"Here, let me help you with that," she told him, leading him to the tiny bathroom in the corner of the cage. When he got in and closed the door, there was barely enough room for him to turn around so he placed the clothes over the small sink. He pulled the lid of the toilet down and sat on it, bringing his hands up to run them through his hair. He felt something new on his hand. Since when had he worn a ring? What on earth was going on? His parents were behaving very strangely. He tried to remember what the last thing he could recall was. Closing his eyes, his hand went out in front of him and felt around an imaginary steering wheel. He could almost feel the car beneath him and the purr of the engine in his ears. Yes, driving. He had been driving. Then he could picture Corey and a black car. But he seemed different. Normally, he would have been friendly and welcoming, but this Corey seemed angry and distant. What had happened between them? What had he done? He couldn't remember.

Shaking his head, he got up and started pulling on the new clothing. It felt stiff and uncomfortable, and he wondered if it had come straight from a rack. It didn't feel like it had even been laundered, which seemed odd. How much preparation could have possibly been done if they had to buy a brand new suit that day? And where had the ring come from? As he pulled the pre-knotted tie over his head, he wondered again to himself what was going on.

CHAPTER THIRTY FIVE

She was hit hard on the side of her head by a massive paw, the claws retracted but the weight of it enough to throw her body completely sideways. For just a fraction of a second, she lost all her orientation as the world spun with stars. But then she felt it, the weight of his body crushing down on hers and trying to pin her in place.

With a terrified yelp, she rolled aside, allowing the pressure to be released and catapulting herself free. Turning her head, she saw the mottled body of Tiny as he prepared to strike again. What the hell was going on?

She tried to call her Alpha powers, but she couldn't feel anything. It was like the switch had been turned off and she was now naked and alone. Terror rattled through her body like a train, sending nerve endings into a spin before her legs dropped low and the propelled her forward. Twisting and turning, she moved in short, sharp bursts, trying to avoid his crushing paws, which she knew were only centimetres from her body. Her head ached, but her lungs were on fire as her brain tried to commit to a path of safety.

A voice was calling her internally—her father.

Submit! He screamed at her, his accent strong and dark. I am your Alpha and I am commanding you to submit!

He wanted her to stop and give in to Tiny, and accept that she was under his pack. Had this been his plan all along? To allow Tiny to take her back with them to America and take control of her, and the rest of the pack? The more he tried to tell her what to do, the faster she ran. The terror of his voice ringing through her ears gave her a speed and agility she didn't know she had.

Darting around, she tried to find a path of escape, even momentarily considering the nearest large tree. But Tiny was hot on her heels, the loud thumps of his paws pushing her on.

Behind her she could hear the frustrated gnash of Tiny's teeth as his paw missed its target once again. Then there was another sound: a low rumble coming from up ahead just past the pond. She froze, just long enough for Tiny to land a blow that sent her tumbling forward.

In the spin, she felt the sharp sting of bracken, but he had again not used his claws. Her wounds were superficial. But behind her, Tiny had applied all the brakes, and slid into a snarling pounce position. She caught her breath as the towering form of a bear came charging through the bush towards them. Sebastian!

With his teeth showing, he bore down on them, and Nicci had to curl slightly to avoid getting crushed in his path. As the bodies of the two men collided, there was a sickening thud and the ripping and tearing of flesh and teeth. They twisted and tore at each other like vipers. Tiny sank his fangs into Sebastian's left front leg, resulting in a horrific roar of pain from the bear's throat. With a twist to his body, Sebastian flung his right paw around and Tiny caught the full force across the side of his head. The momentum sent him toppling, as Sebastian turned to stand up on his back legs and roared down at the now wounded and bleeding Tiny.

But rather than give in, Tiny narrowed his eyes, and with a low growl he jumped forward again, this time trying to go for his throat. With his teeth bared and claws extended he almost reached his target. But despite his size, Sebastian was quick, and dropped down suddenly, pushing his full weight heavily onto him. There were snapping sounds as Tiny screeched and gurgled, and Nicci got to her feet. Tiny wasn't moving at all. Sebastian opened his mouth and roared down at him, before throwing his right paw out and hurtling him across the ground and hard into the side of the tree. The body slumped to the bottom of the trunk, not even registering further injury, and Nicci knew without even having to check that Tiny was already dead.

Sebastian, down on all fours, growled one more time before he turned and looked at Nicci. She could see the total darkness in his eyes, and she took a step back. Blood oozed from his wounds, and his large jaw slackened, showing his wide mouth and bloodied teeth. Staring at him, she wondered if she needed to run. She couldn't see anything left of him, of Sebastian, inside this beast. It was as if the bear had completely taken over.

But then there was a sound, a groan, from deep inside its mouth and she saw the massive head shake as if he were fighting to get back control.

Shivering, she lowered her head at him, hoping that it would be enough to calm the beast and bring Sebastian back. If I can just get through to him somehow.

His head flew up and his back arched, the shimmer of a transformation engulfing him and she heard the sound of bones settling and re-sorting themselves, and his grunt of pain in the process. She allowed herself a moment to gather her thoughts before she transformed herself, feeling the tightness in her movements as she did so. Tiny might not have meant to hurt her, but she was definitely wounded.

Taking heaving breaths, Sebastian looked across at her, blood now running from his leg and forehead. She hadn't noticed the head injury in his bear form, but as a human, the giant gash that ran from just above his ear down his neck looked horrific. Terrified, she jumped forward, dropping down on her knees to where he lay panting on the ground.

"Sebastian!" She touched his hair and felt him flinch and groan. "God! Are you all right?"

"I'll be fine," he grunted, closing his eyes. "It's just a flesh wound."

But the ground was now starting to get sodden, with the fading red of the sky being replaced with the blood that pooled around his body. Nicci tried to pull him up but he was too heavy for her. "We need to get you to Clare. She will know what to do."

He shook his head, his eyes looking up into her own. There was a softness there and she felt again the warm and soft pull of the tendrils of his love unravelling themselves into her mind. She couldn't bring herself to admit that he might be dying. It couldn't happen. Nobody knew her the way he did, and she couldn't let go of those memories. She couldn't let go of him.

"No," he replied quietly, simply. He reached up, his large hand cupping the side of her face like a massive mitt, and stroked her cheek. His skin was rough and calloused, but soft and careful. It was so much of the man himself in his hands.

"How did you find me?" she asked, trying to keep him distracted while the light started to dull in his eyes. No, her brain screamed, he can't go! Keep him distracted, don't let him leave!

"Willow," he murmured. "But I could always find you, kitten."

Nicci could feel the sting of tears in her eyes. He couldn't die! Not Sebastian! Memories wound themselves around them both, as she recalled meeting him for the first time. How scared she had been of the sheer size of him, and how careful and tender he was with her when she was first learning how to work the kitchen. He was the first person she'd opened up to about her past and what she was, and no matter how bad she felt, he always cheered her up.

"Remember when I last found you and we went swimming?" His voice was getting low and faint, but he gave her a soft smile. She wanted to shake him and bring him around, but he looked unusually fragile and pale. Every staggered breath he made chipped away at her own until she felt like her chest was unable to expand.

"Yeah." She tried to smile back, but now the tears were running down her cheeks in long, hot streams and dropping onto his body. "I'll never forget it." Her voice was tight and scratchy. She reached out and cupped his face like he had hers, her heart breaking as she formed the next words. "I'll never forget you."

"Good," he replied, giving off a soft moan. "Because I lo..."

His voice disappeared and his hand fell down to the ground. Nicci lowered her head, and pressed her lips against his mouth as she felt the last tendril of his mind disappear softly into the universe.

He was gone.

CHAPTER THIRTY SIX

His parents had set up a sort of matrimonial decoration in the gardens, and as Dru emerged from the darkness of the basement, his eyes took a while to adjust to the bright light and work out where they were. Caitlin, his nasty ex-girlfriend was there, and he could feel her scowling at him even from this distance, but he chose to ignore her. He doubted that he had invited her, but he didn't recall inviting anyone. Maybe his mother had? People in white uniforms bustled around with drinks and food on trays, but there were very few guests. A handful of chairs had been set up in a row leading up to the arch, and amongst them sat the familiar faces of his father's most loyal pack members. But their faces were grim, their brows tight, and their lips pulled hard. Despite the floral arrangements, this was not a celebration.

Ahead, Corey stood next to Michael. Both men seemed deep in conversation, their heads close together and frowns upon their faces. They turned as he got closer. Rather than giving him the usual friendly greeting, they stopped their conversation and simply stared at him. He rolled the ring on his finger around and around, wondering why it felt so strange and new.

"Hey Corey, Michael." Dru stepped forward.

"Dru," Corey replied, his eyes scanning his face.

Dru frowned. What was that about?

"Hey, bro." Michael looked at him with an unusual expression. "Mum said you had been unwell?"

"Yeah, apparently." He politely declined a glass of champagne that a young girl in white offered him before she scuttled off again. "Bit weird these last couple of days, if I'm honest."

Corey's eyes sharpened. "So did you get in trouble at all?"

"For what?" Dru replied, giving a shrug. "Driving the car? Sorry, I've been unwell, so I don't really remember what's been going on."

Corey frowned. "No, for..." He was clearly about to allude to something, but then his mouth clamped shut.

"For what?" Dru asked again.

"Yes, Corey." Dru felt the rumble of his father's voice by his shoulder and involuntarily flinched. "Do tell? What would Dru possibly be in trouble for? After all, he's just been here with us the whole time, hasn't he?"

There was a low growl to his voice, and Dru turned to look at him.

"Have I been somewhere?" he asked, not able to shake the feeling that he was missing the point of this whole story.

"Not at all," Corey replied, and Dru turned to catch him straightening himself and give him a smile.

It was the same sort of smile that Ashley had been giving him. There was something wrong, he knew it, but he just couldn't work out what. God, if only his head would stop pounding, he was sure that he could figure it out. He raised his hand up to his face and rubbed his eyes.

"Hey, that's a nice ring." Michael spoke and Dru opened his eyes to stare at his hand.

Dru held out his hand to show his little finger to them. There was a soft gold signet ring there, with a red emerald gem encased in the centre.

"Yeah." He took it between two fingers and rolled it around. In the sunshine, it shimmered and flickered as if it was only partially solid. "I don't recall getting it, but it's nice—"

His father cut him off and glared at Michael. "I gave it to you as a wedding gift last week. You must have forgotten, with your illness. Now come along, boys. It's time to get ready and take your places."

He turned and led them towards the front. Pack marriages were normally a whole-pack affair, and it seemed odd to Dru that this one was so small, but security was always a key factor in his father's planning. Perhaps he was worried about having too many people present when they were all there. After all, it wouldn't be the first time a pack had the male heirs taken out on their wedding day.

Dru tried to muster up a smile and some conversation for Corey while they waited for the girls to arrive, but his friend seemed strained and distant. He kept looking nervously across at Michael and towards the entrance, as if he thought something was about to happen. His parents took their places at the front of the seating just before the music started, and Dru noticed that his mother had a few tears on her cheeks. She didn't seem at all happy about the day, either.

As the band began to play, the girls appeared. Their flowing white gowns were almost matching, but their expressions were anything but. Ashley, her long, blond hair tied carefully into a French braid was smiling broadly. The only time she faltered was the brief moment when her eyes caught Corey's, before she straightened her shoulders and continued her march. But poor Amy looked distraught. She was a pretty little thing, with long, mottled golden locks and dark chocolate eyes. But there was skittishness to her, as if she might flee at any moment. Her eyes darted from left to right, and the bunch of flowers in her hands was visibly shaking as she walked. They got worse as she got closer to the altar, and to Dru's father, who seemed to be staring intently at her.

The brides moved to stand beside their future husbands, and Dru looked down at Ashley, reminded again of how beautiful she was. But the look on her face was one of determination, not love, when she looked up at him. Her chin jutted forward and her eyes were sharpened. This can't be right, he told himself. Beside them, Michael had taken Amy's shaking hands, and was looking down into her face with what Dru could best describe as pity. His was also clearly not a love match.

The preacher began his sermon, and talked about the legacy of pack and the importance of the bonds they shared. The ceremonial blade was presented on a silken cloth, its gleaming edges shimmering under the sun. It was tradition when bonded as mates to make a small slice on the hand, and a silken scarf was bound around them, joining them together symbolically as both blood and kin. Packs would have a legacy blade, one covered in intricate carvings and symbols, which was handed down from each generation to the next. In times of the old ways, it had also been used to make sacrifices for pack. As a child, Dru had been terrified of it, but now as it lay there, he found it strangely beautiful. His fingers lazily played with the new ring on his finger, rolling it around and around. The words of the preacher became vaguer and more echoed as he did so.

"Dru," Ashley whispered at him, bringing his focus back. "Pay attention."

Michael and Amy were now facing each other, his body towards Dru and hers away. There was a strange, hardened look in his eyes as he stared down at the blade that was placed in front of them, as if there was something wrong with it. The last time Dru remembered Michael's face looking that way was as a child, when he had been given a toy he didn't ask for at his birthday, but he had to pretend he liked it anyway. That toy had been a weapon, and his father had insisted that Michael needed to learn to use it, but Michael had always been a pacifist. Now, he stared with that same distaste at another weapon.

As the preacher lifted the blade and passed it to Michael he said the words, "And with this blade you take the body of our pack and make your mark."

Dru's fingers froze on the ring he had been playing with, as Michael's fingers wrapped around the handle. As if in unison, there was movement.

Michael suddenly pushed Amy to the side and then lunged forward towards their father. At the same time, Corey, who had been standing behind him, grabbed at Dru as if to pull him out of the way. The motion caused Dru, whose finger had been wrapped around the ring, to pull it free and he felt a sudden rush of energy, a release, move through his whole body. His head, which had moments ago been pounding with pain, became instantly clearer, as if the skies had parted and the gods had shone their light back on his face.

Beside him, Michael had found his mark, the silver tip of the blade now penetrating like an arrow from the chest of their father. His mouth and eyes were wide with shock, while his mother had moved away, covering a scream from her mouth with her hands. There was a flash of snarls and movement as panthers of all shapes and sizes suddenly morphed and changed, their teeth and claws being released in the process. Ashley stood shocked and wide-eyed at the front, next to a trembling Amy, the two women seemingly rooted to their positions.

Dru shook his head as he felt the transformation take over his body, morphing it back into his cat shape. Beside him he heard Corey's voice yelling, before it turned into a solid growl.

"Find her!" he screamed. "Protect Nowhere!"

And like a dagger in his own chest, he could hear Nicci her crying in his head. His mate was in trouble. He needed to save her. With a swish of his tail and a nod of his head at the snarling Corey, who was protecting the girls, he took off towards the gate.

He only hoped he wasn't too late.

#

CHAPTER THIRTY SEVEN

Nicci didn't know how long she lay there holding Sebastian's body. Grief consumed her every cell, and rolled around in her stomach, making her feel nauseous. Unable to let him go, her skin was now soaked in his blood and she could feel him getting colder to the touch. She begged with the gods to bring him back. She promised them they could have anything they wanted, but nothing happened. He didn't move. There would be no more comfort to be found in his arms.

Eventually, she heard the sound of someone approaching at speed, but in her grief she couldn't even try to defend herself. Instead, she lowered her head down to his silent chest and lay awaiting her fate. If they wanted to take her, they could have her. There was nothing left in this world. Her best friend had died. The man she loved had abandoned her. There was nothing left of her shredded heart to take.

A soft hand touched her shoulder, and she raised her eyes.

"Hello, love." Gloria gave her a sad smile, and reached out to tuck a strand of hair behind her ear. The motherly nature of it made her start to sob, and so Gloria, despite her diminutive size bundled her up and into her arms, letting her cry into her shoulder.

Behind them, she could hear other footsteps, and expletives as they uncovered the scene. Then there was a wail. Low and deep, it rumbled through their bodies and she looked through her tear-streaked eyes across at Jakob, bent down over the broken shape of Tiny's panther form. Another stab of pain shot through her as she realised she had also lost family that day. Her breath caught.

Gloria, sensing her body tense, called out.

"Mark! Boys! Go find her something to cover herself with, please. Clare? Are you there?"

Soft footsteps came up closer.

"Go and check on Tiny for us, please, darling, just in case." Her voice was sad and low.

Over Gloria's shoulder, Nicci watched Clare move over to Jakob. It felt like she was watching a movie, rather than seeing people she knew. Sounds were distant, and her brain was struggling to manifest the reality of the situation.

Jakob's head was lowered and his body shook as Clare's hand reached out to his shoulder and their gazes caught. Something in his eyes looked almost wild, but as his own hand reached out and covered the back of Clare's, his face softened. Clare reached down to place her other hand on Tiny, and then gave Jakob a sad shake of her head. He stood up, wrapping his arms around her body and pulling her close. The whole scene rolled out like a silent movie. They never said a word to each other.

She pulled back from Gloria but didn't look down at Sebastian. She couldn't bring herself to see him like that.

Callum returned to the group, running and holding a shawl in his hands, and behind him followed Willow, her long, lean limbs moving silently across the ground.

"Here you go, Mum." Callum passed Gloria the shawl and she pulled it around Nicci's shoulders. It felt warm and comforting.

Willow's eyes were on Nicci's face as she got close, her shoulders heaving from the exercise.

"I'm so sorry," she panted out. "I didn't mean for this to happen. Something changed and I couldn't see anything ahead. It was like you went blank for a while. I was scared for you so I asked Sebastian to come and find you while I went to get backup from the pack, just in case..."

Her eyes dropped past Nicci and down to the torn body at her feet, and her face grew pale. She turned her head away.

"It's not your fault." Nicci's voice sounded quiet and distant, even to herself. There was a total lack of emotion to it, as if she were a computer giving instructions. But her body had begun to shake.

"Let's get you back to the pack." Gloria's eyes were darting around in the shadows. "We have managed to fight off most of the attackers, and we think that the last of them might be fleeing, but it's better to be safe than sorry."

Nicci turned to look down at the mangled corpse next to them.

"But Sebastian..." she muttered, her heart filling again with sadness as she saw his vacant face.

"He's gone now, love." Gloria reached out and pulled her chin to face her. "You can't do anything about him right now. You need to be the Alpha. Your pack needs you."

Nicci swallowed. Gloria was right. It was time for her become the leader that they needed, and prove herself worthy of their loyalty.

Her pain had made her feel numb, but now she could feel it etching into her bones. He did this. It was his fault. Closing her eyes she called out to her father, the growing anger in her about what he had done building up and erupting.

"You have not won," she snarled. "You do not control me and you are not my Alpha. I will no longer even recognise you as my father. You are nothing to me. I am stronger than you, and I am better than you. You have no power over me."

She heard his hiss and the gnash of his teeth in reply before she cut off the sounds of him in her head. Like turning off a switch, he was gone.

Opening her eyes, she found that the group around her had cast their heads down, as if bowing to her. Jakob was the first to look up.

"What would you like us to do?" he asked.

"I'm not your Alpha," Nicci told him. "You are part of my father's pack, and as such, you can leave whenever you want. But if you choose to stay, you are kin, and I will always treat you as such."

Jakob nodded, his gaze dropping down to Clare, whose head was still lowered. Nicci remembered when the two of them had first met, after he had been injured by Corey, and wondered if they had harboured feelings for each other all this time? Had Nicci been naïve about everything, or had she chosen not to see the truth of things?

"I will stay," he said.

Her eyes flew up to meet his own, and hold them.

Nicci could still feel the anger inside of her. Where the sadness had been, a raging torrent was growing and churning. Outsiders had come to hurt her pack—her family. Even her blood relatives had tried. She had enough of men trying to control her, and take from her. It was time for vengeance. Her father would be on the list, but first she needed to ensure that the local packs knew that she was not to be messed with.

"Gloria." She turned to look at the older woman, who was now frowning back at her. "Please take your family and the others, and get back to the safety of the pack. Jakob and I have work to do."

Giving her a small nod, Gloria's lips pulled tight. "Just be careful," she warned. "These are dangerous creatures you are dealing with."

"I know." Nicci swallowed. She watched as Jakob reached out and gave Clare a small squeeze on her hand, before they started to depart. When Willow got just beyond the clearing she reached out, and lifted up the broken necklace. Raising it high, she called out to Nicci.

"What do you want me to do with this?"

"Hold on to it," Nicci replied. "It might come in useful someday."

Willow nodded, waving her hand across it until it suddenly disappeared. She turned and gave Nicci the thumbs up before continuing on her way.

Looking across at Jakob, Nicci noticed that his shoulders had squared and his jaw was tight.

"Feel like going hunting?" she asked him, shaking free of her human form and welcoming the simmering pain of the transformation. As her sleek, dark paws hit the ground, she stretched out her claws.

"I thought you'd never ask," he growled, and joined her.

#

CHAPTER THIRTY EIGHT

When Willow got back to the township, she could feel it burning and searing the very flesh within her.

Gloria turned and looked back, giving her a small frown as the rest of her family moved swiftly towards the shelters.

"Are you okay, Willow?" she asked.

"I'm fine. I just need to take care of something," Willow grunted, the sharp sting of it now radiating out along her limbs.

"Okay, well don't be long," Gloria replied, her eyes darting out to watch for movement. "It's still not safe here yet, you know."

Oh, she knew all right. Images swirled around her vision. Screams. Cries. There were two dark panthers, moving as if in simultaneous unison, the blood of their fallen victims spattered across their faces and chests. The chants of the mages, some of them friends of hers that she had trained with, were drowned out by gurgling as their throats were ripped open and their magic failed. She tried to swallow down the bile that rose to her mouth.

Staggering as another sharp stabbing pain hit her chest, she gasped. She needed to get this thing out of her before it killed her.

Getting as far into the woods as she dared, she drew forth her summoning powers and muttered the sacred words. Raising her hands skyward, she gave the final signal, and the necklace that she had found down by the lake presented itself, removed from the inner canvas of her magical powers. The relief of getting it free made her knees buckle. Dropping to the group, she ran a finger over one of the stones and felt the blue hellfire within it flicker and churn.

She had only ever heard of the hellfire stones, a rumour of witchcraft that had been passed down through the aeons, from one mage to another. Now, here she was with the very things themselves, casually underneath her fingertips She couldn't believe that it had been so easy, in the end. Nicci was naïve in the ways of the magical world. Had they fallen into the hands of any other pack, her participation on the attack of Nowhere tonight would have cost her life. Perhaps the gods had greater things planned for her than she knew. Clasping her fingers around the stones, she planted her other hand deep into the soil next to her body, and closed her eyes, uttering a summons.

"Goddess of Earth, I call on you. Give my gifted sight a sign of where these stones came from. Show me the gateway for which they protect. Guide me, my goddess."

She felt a shudder roll through her body, and then a sharp tearing sting like a thousand bees hitting her instantly. She threw her head back and allowed the images to form in her mind. Fleeting pictures, of both past and present, melded themselves, flashing through like a slide show. Shifters, mages, humans. She recognised Nicci, and saw her taking the stones from a table, the stones responding to her very touch. All manner of creatures had found these stones through the ages, but all the finders shared one similar thing. They had all subsequently made their way to the source location.

These stones had come from Nowhere.

As the show stopped, Willow's eyes flew open.

This was the gateway which the stones protected, the gateway she had sought for so long. And now she was right in the heart of it.

A smile crossed her lips.

It was time.

CHECK OUT ANOTHER VK TRITSCHLER STORY!

What happens when two lost were-panthers meet for the first time?

Nicci, a were-panther abandoned as a child and without a pack, finds herself on the run from the law. With nothing left to lose, she doesn't trust anyone, especially her own heart.

Dru, a famous race car driver and inheritor of one of the most influential packs in Australia, is trying to escape notoriety, and his fate. Prepared to throw away everything, he is trusting his instincts to get him through.

Together they find themselves stuck in a small rundown deserted town called Nowhere in the wilderness of rural Australia.

Can they learn to trust each other and find a future, or is the call of the wild too strong?

ABOUT THE AUTHOR

VK Tritschler is the definition of very busy. Having both a fulltime job, a growing family and a career as an author she has a lot going on both around her and in her imagination. She lives on the amazing Eyre Peninsula in South Australia, having moved there from her hometown of Christchurch, New Zealand. Her family consists of a very patient husband, two rampant boys, and too many pets to mention.

Ever available to her readership you can find her at:

http://www.vktritschler.com

http://www.facebook.com/vktritschler

http://www.twitter.com/vktritschler

http://www.goodreads.com/vktritschler